# Our Love

Raven! Yes Ravon! Since we promised Gramma Rhonda we would write a book about her and G Pa love towards each other. How ironic is it that she died 5yrs and 5 days after him. I know it's still hurting to know that she's no longer with us. I was looking forward to being with the family at Christmas having fun instead we we're there because auntie Calven had found her lying across her bed holding onto G Pa's pic.

 I wish I could've been there to say goodbye to her one last time Ravon. I know she was such a loving person that was able to fall in love again after all those years of being abused. Yes she did, what was her joke she used to say Raven? You mean I married the first time for love the second time will be for money not knowing it wasn't the money it was the love and a big dick. Yep! She was so damn nasty but kept it real about everything in her life. Yes G Pa said life began for him again when Rhonda Simpson came back into his life for good.  What did he used to say she came back Just In Time? I believe that's the reason why he always sang that song around the house as well as Lately. I'll tell you my dad sings it just as beautiful as G Pa.

But I don't want to hear it out of him no time soon. He just sang it at Uncle Dwayne's funeral then about 6 weeks later at his mother's own funeral well I mean step-mothers funeral. Now you no if Gramma Rhonda was still alive she would've cussed your ass out for calling her, his stepmother. Ya you got that right; I can hear her calling you big head high yella heffa if you don't cut that shit out I'll whip your ass if you call me that one more time.

Well I think we should start off with Just In Time: because it was his song even though it was a gospel song it meant a lot to the both of them. With all the pain and turmoil that the both of them went through. Even though it was a new century let alone a different time they were shunned upon because of their race him being African-American and her being Italian and Greek. An eggplant and a greaser aren't supposed to be together.

So it was Just In Time that kept their love together. Yes cuz! So you gonna sing it or me? I'll do it because I've heard you sing before Ravon not being mean or not saying you can't sing but damn you hurt my ears when I do hear you singing. Now that's messed up to say to me cuz. But I like your honesty. Question do you think any of the family will be interested in helping write this book?

Yes I was talking to VJ3 at the funeral and he said he wanted to help as much as possible. Cool! Just In Time, Jesus stepped in time, Not a moment, He was not moment to late, God was not a moment to soooooooooon, He was Just Ohhhh He was Just, Just In Time, Just In Time, Just Before All My Hope Was Gone, Just In Time Just before faith walked out the door, Just In Time right when I needed him the most, He was he was just oh thank you lord you were Just In Time, Just In Time, right before all my hope was gone.

Raven that was beautiful but I'm like you now I really don't want to hear that song no time soon either. I can't believe she's no longer with us though? I had the pleasure to sit down with her just before thanksgiving of last year to shoot the breeze and go through some old journals that she was keeping to write her life story. I told her I would love to write it along with her help.

She was overly excited about the project and couldn't wait to start working with me, but wanted to make sure it was done in a way that showed her love for James as well as G Pa. What kept you from doing it when we were all here at thanksgiving? Nothing we spent a few nights brainstorming over titles and how to start it off when she decided to call it Our Love. That's very simple but pretty Raven!

Yes it is she wanted to call it this because it was their love but Our Love as a family that made her life happy. Well since V3 is still here why don't we game plan this as well as get started on the project because with the 3 of us doing this we might be able to have it finished by her birthday March 6th. True indeed. V3 can you come here for a minute we have something to ask you?

Yes Ravon, what's up cuz? Remember when we were talking about finishing Gramma and G Pa's book? Yes but we never started it so how can we finish it Raven? Why do you have to be such a smart ass? I'm not a smart ass I'm a very intelligent black male get it right. Well excuse me mister college professor. Okay enough you two I don't understand how y'all can be brother and sister an act like an ole married couple.
It's easy Ravon; just like how you and your twin fight all the time she thinks she's older than me and smarter but she so so wrong. I'm the oldest grandchild so you might say I'm honored to be a part of this since I was around them the most. Yes you can tell us what it was like back when they were dating and how both families came together as one?

Yes and then some how the woman I always thought was my biological grandmother really wasn't to finding out that gramma was my grandfather's first and true love but do to unforeseen circumstances they never got married until later on in life. So since you brought that up V3 how did you feel when you found out that Gabi nor Rhonda weren't your biological grandmother?

Ravon it's complicated to explain but after meeting my biological grandmother once I became and adult I'm glad that I had the latter two in my life in that role. Gramma Gabi instilled in me as well as my sister's the power of education and that we could be whatever we wanted in life, and Gramma Rhonda believed in love once she let all of her old barriers down and let G Pa completely into her life once again, she showed all of us that thinking of others feelings and not thinking we're better than others we just happen to have a Patriarch that worked hard to build a business that's on its 3$^{rd}$ generation of Martin's running it.

That's true but did it anger you that G Pa didn't marry your grandmother or that she didn't want to be in your life or your mothers? Mommy always had problems with that because she had the loving father that carried for her deeply and a stepmother that raised as her own but when it came time for her to connect with her biological mothers side of the family she yearn for that more than anything until Rhonda came back into G Pa's life and she really found out the story behind the family and why she was treated the way she was.

Gabi had explained a little but Rhonda had went more in-depth with her explaining that her mothers family really didn't care to much for her father so he fought to get full custody of her and raised her along with their dogs Winnie and Nelson. After hearing this story from Gramma I grew even closer to my mother than ever. G Pa also explained to me that if it wasn't for Rhonda he would've lost it back then they were both teenagers he was 16 and she was 14 when they met in high school but instantly connected on all different levels from companionship to love that never truly died.

Well I guess that's why they were unbreakable once they got back together? Yes Raven now your getting it, it wasn't about the songs, running around the house naked chasing one another, nor uniting all of us as a family. They never lost love and wanted to show that to all of us regardless if we wanted to hear at the time they where preaching it to us but it never left us. Our love for one another is unstoppable, unbreakable and if you get on our bad side all hell is gonna break loose because if you fuck with one you're fucking with all of us.

Yes a bond that I hope will never be broken by anyone. Girls it won't because I don't want to deal with the wrath of our parents they're a united force when it comes to ass whipping and messing with any of us either. Yes especially your mother, cause Aunt Dayna ain't no joke when it comes to whipping ass. Yes she is because I remember when auntie Calven was dating that girl and she broke bad here I thought for sure bullets were gonna fly. Nah my mom would've beat dat ass but she isn't gonna pull her gun because that's her lively hood. Sis I think your wrong because mommy would use it to protect everyone of us because this woman went from one end of the scale going straight off the deep in.

Calling us nigga's, spear chucker's, and everything else. To be honest I thought mommy was gonna get her, it was Gramma that went to town on her because she didn't want mommy to lose her job. You got that right Gramma was like Dayna baby don't mess your career up I'm old I can do the time for beating this bitches ass.

You had to love her because she's not gonna back down regardless. Our family, our love is one that should be studied by folks because it's truly the United Nations. Not really we're just an amazing family that loves with all of our heart. I remember G Pa would sing this to her in they're Jaguar. You must be talking about lately? Yes I am they would slow drag off of it then I don't know what she would say to him in his ear they would either run to the pool house or goto their room for hours then come out smiling. Yes but did you ever listen to the words?

No, not really! Well let me sing it then for you. Owe Dreams, Dreams of you, I'll do anything to spend a little time with you, the way you turned my world all around feels so good, when I goto sleep late at night all I see girl is you, all I see is you, baby you blow my mind what am I suppose to do. Lately I've been dreamin' to myself and girl I really want you bad.

Yes brotha you betta sing it. Now I get it, it was all about how G Pa loved her and dreamt about her all the time. Yes he dedicated a whole album to her when he was still married to Gabi, that there said a lot about what his feelings were towards her. Do you realize the balls the two of them had being married and running around with one another. I heard a story once either from my mom or Uncle VJ about how her friends almost stopped talking to her because she was with G Pa not because she was cheating on her husband. Of course she was everything from being a nigger lover to a whore.

 It didn't tear her down it actually built her up to be who she was only one that never turned her back on neither one of them was Aunt Donna. But that relationship V3 was more like a sisterhood than anything. Yes that's it; it was a sisterhood bond that was true until the end. She really did well at the funeral. The person I'm still scared for is my dad. Why Raven? Because they were so close after G Pa and nana passed away. They talked at least 3 to 4 times a week.

She trusted him so much that she chose him over your mom to making him our companies CEO and making her the CFO. Well I wouldn't say so much trust Raven it was more like she needed someone there on a daily basis that had that type of attitude of getting shit done without any half stepping. So here's how I feel, we should start the book with if y'all agree. Well shoot then V3! Okay I would love to put my family tribute in the being of it then go into how they taught all of us how to love one another but don't go all trivia about it but tell the story of Our Love.

Now V3 that's the way to do it, it will draw your audience in but we gotta stay on path with it not going all over the place with it because they will put it down and not pick it back up. Raven do you remember where Gramma kept the journals at so we can go through them to start putting it together? Yes I do, V3 didn't you say that G Pa kept notes and words of encouragement in his studio downstairs? Yes if I'm not mistaken uncle VJ said there were stuff like that down there do you want me to look for you guys?

If you could because the more we have the better the story we could tell about Our Love. Whose gonna type this project or are we gonna use a ghostwriter? I'll do it guys! That's what I do for my career so it won't take me any time to get it done after we figure out the concept and getting the structure down pat. V3 do have what you said for the family tribute still handy? Yes I do I don't even need to look at the paper I can say it verbatim. Well go on with your badass professor Martin. Friends and Family on behave of my family I would extend a hardy thank you for coming out to help us celebrate the woman we knew as mother, grandmother, and great-grandmother as well as aunt and friend. I had the pleasure of calling her grandmother, even though she wasn't my biological one. She meant more to me than my real one did because she help raise me from the time I came home from the hospital until her death 5 days ago. Since were on the subject I'm gonna give you the importance of the number 5 and how it pertains to our family. My grandfather passed away 5 years ago and 5 days to the day that my grandmother did he died the 20th of December she died the morning of the 25th. I know that the both of them are in heaven dancing right now but also saying V3 just get to the point because theses folks have a life.

You no what Vic and Rhonda your right, but I had the grand pleasure of being named after him and if y'all remember my G Pa or my Uncle VJ you know that they could get a wall to talk back to them so I guess I'm gonna carry on that torch. Grandma Rhonda treated all of us the same if we got out of hand that ole school Italian and Greek blood would come out. Can I get an Amen on that from my cousins and siblings? Amen V3! We used to joke that she wanted to be black so damn bad that she even beat our butts like she was a black mother.

But in all seriousness to my mother Dayna, my Aunts Robyn, Bree, Calven and Uncles VJ and Jimmy, she might not be here with us in the physical she'll forever live in our hearts. For some crazy reason the two of them could get the whole family together even when we didn't know we had to be together. Grams best friend from childhood Auntie Donna used to joke and say they could make a party out of anything. Which was true when my grandparents moved down here I was about 9 or 10 you know how they got everyone down here to help them unpack and party anyone?

Well I'll tell you my G Pa had a bad reaction to something that had him in the hospital for more than a week to the point they had given him his last rites. But nope it took him a whole 20 years to meet his demise. Theses folks party for about a week or so. In closing gramma thank you for the beatings, thank you for those harsh words when it was needed, thank you for encouraging all of us to strive for the stars, thank you for loving us in a way that will never be replaced, and last but not least thank you for loving Victor the way you did even after his passing he was always your love and you made sure everyone knew this.

I'll be lookin' out my front door for you gramma. If it's all right with y'all can sing a few words of a song I would hear sung around the house it's called Love. Yes V3 going do your thing. Love, a word that comes and goes, but few people really know what it really means to love somebody, Love though the tears may fade away I'm so glad your love will stay cause I love you, and you showed Jesus what it really means to Love. That's all I can say because its hurting my heart.

 I love you Gramma Rhonda Rest In Paradise with G Pa, Nana and your dad. She's finally back with those who truly loved you unconditionally? Oh my God V3 I really didn't listen to it when you spoke at the funeral because I was in such of a state of disbelieve but hearing you saying those words all over again I got chills all through body. Well Raven I was speaking straight from the heart her love scratch that their love for one another was incredible which trickled down to all of us that's why we should call it Our Love, that's the only way to explain it all.

Well I'm all for that name! Ravon you and your sister wanted to do a album of G Pa's music but done as inspirational and religious right? Yes V3 our dad was gonna help us produce it your brother Dayvon wanted to be on it as well. Damn I just got an idea why don't we try to coincide both of them. Sounds like a good one Raven but what do you think auntie Robyn's and uncle Jimmy's kids are going to say? Look were all family so if we're doing it everyone is doing it I'm the oldest grandchild I'll express to them that's what we all want to do and I'm quite sure they'll all jump aboard.

Raven since we're gonna open up with my family tribute I think you should go next with the stories that she shared with you during the time you spent with her at Thanksgiving. Okay but it was kinda of racy what she shared with me. C'mon it couldn't of been no more racy than what we heard and saw growing up around them.

That's what you think guys, this shit is real deep and somewhat nasty. Hell I think we can handle it. Okay don't say I didn't warn your asses? The summer of 1992 I graduated high school, still living at home with my mom who I loved with all my heart. I haven't heard from him and I know his fucking black ass is back from college because not only did Donna tell me she saw him but Bryan did as well. I don't know what kinda of fucking game he's trying to play but if I don't hear from him by the end of the week I'm so damn done.

Are you okay baby? Why mommy? Because I heard you talking to someone or yourself! Yes I was talking to myself about why Victor Martin hasn't contacted me yet and he's been home for over 2 weeks now? Well baby he'll contact soon because he loves him some you. Well excuse me for what I'm getting ready to say.

Fuck him and the ship he came in on. Because if that was so true I should've been the first person he called and came by to see.

Oh my goodness Rhonda I'm so sorry baby. Why are you saying you're sorry for mommy? The other night when you went out on that date with that boy James. Ya mom, Victor called you and I forgot to tell you. Damn! Now he probably thinks I'm being funny or not interested in him. You can clear it up if you just tell him that I forgot to tell you that he had call. Besides it seems like your more interested in this new guy than you are about Vic anyway right? No don't say that I'm keeping my options open.

Well I just have an unsettled feeling about this James boy but its your life and your 18 now so I cant tell you what to do only thing I can do is to tell you to be careful. Your father and I will stand behind you regardless of what you may choose to do. Now mom do you think daddy wants Victor in the family?

I'm gonna tell you this one thing about your father and don't you go repeating it either. He acts like this big bad ass but he's a sucka for his Bree Bell ie… Rhonda he'll be happy with whoever you choose but he's gonna act hard because that's what a father is suppose to act towards his daughter's gentlemen callers. Mom really that sounds so crazy to me. It might sound country but it's the truth. I hope so because if I choose Victor I hope he'll love him just as much as you do. Now that I can't promise you that but I know he will respect your wishes.

Mommy I'm fresh out of high school starting my adult life college and working. I want a lot out of life, you and daddy have set the bar high for any man to get me and to keep me as well so if you were a betting person who would you put your money on James or Victor and when you give your response go into detail for your ya and nay? It's a no brainer for me Rhonda that would be Victor and here's the reasons why, 1.) He's very intelligent, 2.) I have a feeling deep down inside he's gonna be famous 3.) He is well-mannered 4.) He can dress his ass off 5.) Last but not least I know you've seen how his pants fit in front? Now why not James?

Well I'm gonna be blunt and to the point he's trash and judging by his attitude he looks like he's abusive. I'll kill a muthafucka if they ever got it messed up that they could put their hands on you Rhonda. Mommy I would hope that he wouldn't do that if I decided to be with him. Boy was gramma so right about that. Nana knew all the way back then that James was a piece of shit. Yes she did! But let me finish guys you'll see how long this was really going on before it really happened. Mommy if I page Victor can he come by to see me? Girl you don't have to ask me that he can come over anytime, just respect my house like you respect his mother's house.

If it gets hot and bothered I hope y'all are using protection? Yes mom of course I don't want to be a mother at this age. Besides he already has that beautiful daughter of is Dayna. Now that's something else I wanted to ask you? Yes mom! You don't see anything wrong with him having a daughter? Mom that was before me and to be honest with you with him being in school away from his daughter he makes up every minute when he is home.

I'm totally cool with him being a father, I don't have to worry about her mother either because if he has her with him when he picks me up he'll let me know ahead of time so I'll no to be on my best behavior when we drop her off. One time her mother was walking out of her parent's house to get her and was talking shit to me calling me the new white whore in his life. I quickly corrected her ass, I told her you might be a whore or allow men to call you that but I'm not one and my parents didn't raise me that way so you can go fuck yourself.

That was kinda harsh Rhonda but I understand why you went there with her. She got little snippy with me after saying that, this chick had the nerve to say to me that I better be careful because he'll get your white ass pregnant and leave you too. Trust me no good white respectful man wants you after you have a nigger's baby. Wow I had to put the brakes on this chick because first of all he wasn't all that when you were screwing him on a regular basis. In fact you 2 were very happy up until you found out about me talking to your babies father.

You didn't say all that Rhonda did you? Mommy I sure did because he means that much to me but with him all the way at Bethune-Cookman College in Daytona Beach, its so hard for me to trust him I don't think he would cheat on me nor has he. But I'm not sure if his love is true. Who's that Rhonda? What do you mean mom? A car just pulled in front of the house. I'll go look out the living room window. Okay I'm gonna go and use the ladies room while you do that. I can't tell who it is but it's a corvette. Maybe it's your father he's probably having another mid life crisis.

Nope I no who it is mommy! Then who the hell is then? It's Victor; can I go out with him if he wants to go out? Boy how we've changed our tune in just a few short hours. Stop it mommy, I don't want him thinking I was talking shit about him. Okay I let you swear before because you were so upset. But now you have to chill with that language you understand. Yes ma'am! Well look who decided to come and see his girlfriend after being home for 2 weeks. Yes Rhonda if you check with your mom you'll see that I called you but you didn't call me back so I had to come by and see what was up. So are you gonna take me for a ride in that sexy ass car your driving? Yes after I speak to your mother we can. Okay because I have a surprise for you and I hope you like it. Rhonda just being in your presences is more than enough for me.

Really Vic, theres no need to get all corny on me. I'm not, I was thinking if your not doing anything this weekend would you like to go with me to Great Adventures I wanna take Dayna, it's my weekend with her? Sure I'll have to ask my mom if it's okay? Well you can ask her now that way I'll no to get two rooms or at least double beds. No need to get another room because if I go we're gonna be like it's suppose to be. Hey mommy Victor is here he wants to see you. Stop all that damn yelling Rhonda.

I'm coming! Hello Mrs. Waters and how is the most beautiful mother-in-law doing? Victor stop it your not married to my daughter. Not yet but someday I'll be and I'll still feel that way about you. You're a smooth talker you remind me of this guy I was dating when I was college. Really! How is that ma'am was he black like me? To be exact he was and the best lover I ever had. His name was RayVern. So is that where I get the love of the black male from mommy? Nah I taught you that color isn't an issue but judging one on his color is. Okay I have something to ask you Mrs. Waters? What is it Victor? I have my daughter this coming weekend and I'm taking her to Great Adventures I would like for Rhonda to accompany us there if that's all right with you? Well your both are young adults and I hope if your gonna do anything that you'll use protection?

Ma'am I'm not gonna lie to you I do want to have sex with her but my young daughter will be there so I'll doubt if anything like that will be going on. Well if y'all decide to do that just be careful please. We will. So I can go mommy? Yes Rhonda you can. Thanks mommy you just made my week. What time do I have to be home tonight? Be home before 2 please so I'll be able to sleep tonight. I'll have her home by then ma'am. Thanks Victor, how are your parents doing? I haven't seen your mom in a few months, we would bump into each other at the store every once and awhile.

They're doing pretty good, my dad is retiring this year and my mom is still with the bank. Tell her I said hey, and we should get together for drinks or something. I will ma'am I'll have Rhonda home by 2 as you requested. Victor before you leave, don't ever break my babies' heart or mine because we both care about you a lot. I promise you ma'am I'll never do that to you or to her. Bye mommy! Have fun but not too much. We will ma'am. Damn I thought you would never stop talking Victor Martin. So whose corvette is this or did you steal this? Nah it's my big brothers he's visiting and let me drive it tonight.

It must be nice to drive whatever you want? Rhonda why do you always go there babe, I wanted to chill with you not argue with you because I would never win anyway because of that hot ass

Mediterranean blood that runs through your body. Yep, you wouldn't but I'm not gonna do that because I wanna taste your cock in my mouth. Really girl your gonna go there, no how was this semester, did you miss me Victor? Nope I'll ask you all that when I'm done. Well how have you've been doing, I'm sorry I wasn't able to get back in time to go with you to your senior prom.

Don't worry about it, I went with a family friend and nothing went on either before you ask me okay. I guess I missed out twice on going to a prom with you. Yes you did but the important thing is that we're together now aren't we? Yes Rhonda we are but for how long? I called you 2 days after I got back home and you didn't get back to me nor did you page I made sure that Donna saw me and told her to let you know I'm home. Well about that my mom had forgotten to tell me until tonight when I was going off about you not coming to see me and as far as Donna she just told me that she had seen you and said hello.

Well it seems like folks don't want us to be together Rhonda? Victor please don't say that regardless what may happen in our future you'll never be out of my life do you hear me. I hear you but even that statement is saying a lot without you saying anything. My question to you is if your not happy or you want to date other people please let me know Rhonda? Remember what you used to say Victor R Martin, gets what he wants regardless of whom maybe in his way? Yes all of us girls said that about you, and it's so true. Victor you would be the first one to no if I was seeing someone else or if my feelings have changed towards you.

Hey Victor turn that up please. Why Whitney Houston? Just turn it up and you'll see and I'll sing it for you. I've found out what I've been missin', always on the run, I've been lookin for someone, Now you're here like you've been before and you know just what I need, It took sometime for me to see, That you give good love to me Victor, So good take my heart and promise you won't hurt me. Damn Rhonda I never knew you could sing like that, someday your gonna be famous. Ya right, your just saying that because you want me to sing on your microphone. Girl that's not something I'm looking for from you but if you want to slob on the knob I'm not gonna stop you either.

So Victor I'm thinking about getting a seasonal job with the government should I do it? Which division are you looking into and what about school? Well the social security department is hiring for the summer as a clerk and I need the money, as far as college goes I'm going to Post my major is gonna be international law. That's cool, I thought you wanted to come and be with me at Bethune-Cookman? I do but I know that's gonna be hard for my mother to pay for school out of state. I think you found somebody else but that's cool if you did. Victor stop being such a freaking cornball.

I'm not I just got a feeling but I might be wrong. Hey did I tell you that you're a strong, positive woman that any man would be happy to have as their girl or even just as a friend. That's so sweet Vic! Now since you had forty questions with me it's my time? Did you cheat on me while you were at school or were you stroking off thinking about my tight Greek and Italian body rubbing up against yours? I went on a couple dates but I had already told you about those girls. Yes you did Victor and I like that you were totally honest with me, you don't know how much that makes me feel appreciated that you don't have to lie to me.

Rhonda like I've told you from day one I'm here until they throw dirt on my black ass and I mean that. I love you Victor so damn much why cant we be a little older because I would so get married to you without even thinking about it. Now you know damn well you don't mean that? Yes I do Victor with you I feel wanted, loved, and cared for you don't look at me as a sex object or even a stupid person you value my opinion as well as listening to me when no one else will. Our love is unbreakable babe. What did you just say Rhonda? What do you mean what did I just say Victor? The thing you said about our love being unbreakable.

Yes I meant it when I said those words. Look in my eyes Victor before I kiss you and do what I said I want you to look into my hazel eyes and repeat theses words please. Okay I will Rhonda. Our love is unbreakable and that we'll forever be in each other's life regardless of what life throws at us. Do you really mean this Rhonda? What if I marry that crazy black woman that doesn't understand our relationship? Like I said regardless I'm gonna be there for you Victor.

Since you brought that up what if I marry an abusive man that gets off beating me will you safe me? Not only will I safe you but I will try with everything in my power to take care of that poor soul that used you as a punch bag. Hold the fucking phone guys are you reading this? Yes Raven, duh! No I'm not being funny but it's almost like they knew they were gonna end up together in the future. That's what it looks like, when was this notebook started by gramma? It says 6/1992-3/1993! Damn that means they've been planning this for a lifetime.

Yes they have V3 it's scary if you ask me. Not one bit it's showing us right here how deep their love was for one another and they would always be there until the end. Well this is getting really good so lets shut up and get back to it. Now where was I at before y'all stopped me? Gramma was saying something about her marrying someone that would abuse her would G Pa saving her. Okay I found my spot. Victor I wouldn't want you to do all that. Damnit Rhonda I'm not gonna let you go through all that and not have any fun do you understand me? Yes Vic, remember I was just saying what if, because I'm gonna be married to you anyway.

We'll have the pretty house with the picket fence and our beautiful bi-racial children, have full custody of Dayna as well because I'll be a better mother to her than her own mother. Shit she's crazy about me as it is right now. Yes she is, she's the reason why I asked you to come because she asked me to ask you. I can't wait to spoil her little butterball self. Here's our favorite spot to sit and watch the waves and stare up at the sky. Yes it is do you want to get out and go for a walk on the beach before you do that?

Yes only if you give me a piggyback ride. For you I think I can arrange that. Rhonda you complete me babe I promise you that'll never change the way that I am. I'm all for that Vic. So do you want a big wedding or a small one? It doesn't matter to me because it's all about the bride anyway I'm there just as figurehead and to provide fun on the wedding night. True but I would want your input if we were to get married Vic.

Well I would make it a party that folks would still be talking about 20 years later. I do have to say that about you Leo's y'all believe in having a damn good time for days. Yes we do. I love how the water sounds at night coming to ashore it's so peaceful here. Yes it is, so how many bitches have you've gone to the beach with while at school? Just those two I told you about and I will swear on both of my grandfather's graves we didn't do one thing.

I'm serious about us, that's why I said if your not sure about us and our relationship I would understand. I wouldn't hate you nor do anything to jeopardize our friendship because that's more important to me than hating you or whomever your with. Victor your so fucking amazing sometimes I ask myself is this for real or not? Then you go and say or do something like this that just melts my heart. Our love is a bond that wont be broken by anyone. Well I would hope so Rhonda.

It's getting kinda of late and I promised your mother I would have you home by 2 am it's almost one now and I'm not gonna drive my brothers corvette fast to get you home. Okay but I still owe you that special gift I promised you. Yes I remember but how about this Rhonda, instead of you doing that you owe me, because if you do that you won't be home on time. Why is that Vic? Because I haven't had sex since when I was home in December when we got the room down at the Holiday Inn. Now you're lying to me Vic right?

Nope I haven't done anything not even whacking off. We'll see this weekend won't we? Yes Rhonda, this song right here I would dedicate to you at least when I was on the air it got me through the tough times. Just listen to the words, Won't you take a little time now that you no how I feel, don't need no lie detector to see I'm for real, I want you bad wow won't you do like you do late at night when I'm dreaming about. Victor do you really think of me that way or are you pulling my leg?

Just like your crazy about You Give Good Love To Me, by Whitney Houston well that song right there does the same for me. Holy shit guys we are actually reading what happened to their relationship. I see why they were so much in love with one another. Yes but I want to get to the part when she meet James and started dating him. That's coming Dayvon trust me it's coming. Well I cant believe Vic its time for you to leave again. Yes Rhonda we had a lot of fun this summer I can't wait to see when I come home for thanksgiving.

I no! Remember what I told you Victor about our love? It's unbreakable regardless what may come between us you'll always be right there. I will keep that in my heart girl. What time are y'all leaving in the morning? I think my dad is pulling out of here around 8 or 9 why? Because I wanna see you, is that okay with you? Yes I was trying to figure out away how I could see you myself. I'll be there at 8:30 after I drop my mom off at work. Okay I'll see you then love you Rhonda! Love you too Vic. Hey Donna! What's up Rhonda?

I thought you would be with your baby before he leaves to go back to school. I was with him in fact my baby just left me. So Rhonda y'all are still together I see. Yes why wouldn't we Donna? I love me some Victor. That maybe true but what about that dude James you've been talking about? What about him, he's just a nice guy that I've been on a few dates with. To be honest with you he's really not my type of guy I'm not really into the racing thing or wrestling either. I like cultural shit that Vic and I do music concerts, museums, food tasting.

That might be true but I see you talking more about him then Victor. He must be doing something that Vic isn't or is he a feel-in for Victor while he's at college? No my heart is with Victor. Well girl I'm gonna ask you the same thing in a few weeks and see what your response is, if you do decide to be with this James Simpson make sure you don't lead Victor on because he's such a sweet guy to you and he deserves that respect. Yes I will Donna, but trust me I'm not gonna do that to him.

Hold on I'm getting another call. Okay but hurry cause I'm getting ready to goto bed. Ya, Ya, Ya….. Okay I'm back! So who was that on the phone? I'm not gonna say because your not going to jump down my throat. Yep my boy Victor hasn't even left the state and your already cheating on him let me rephrase that having fun. Donna don't judge me, like Victor ain't chasing tale while he's away at school? Rhonda um no! Remember he came home and told you he went on two dates while there, shit he didn't even whack off because he thought was like cheating on you. I'm just ashamed of you right now because he's done so much for you.

Girl I know I'm just exploring my options, besides when guys do it it's okay but when a female does it we're whores or sluts. Yes that's what they call us, but I'm telling you don't hurt him Rhonda please? We've known each other since 2nd grade I can remember when your parents were going through their divorce you didn't understand what it all meant when you found out that I went through the same thing we connected with one another and I've never gave you any bad advice have I? No you haven't Donna! So why won't you listen to me about this particular situation? I'm listening and I'm telling you that nothing is going on between the two of us.

But I really know you Rhonda and your wishing I would just shut up and say goodnight so you can call him back. You know what Donna I really hate you right about now bitch? That's not nice to say to me. Well because I was just thinking how I could get you off the phone so I could call James. Yep! Well goodnight, I can't believe your actually doing this? Don't blame me if shit goes sore between Victor and you. I won't Donna I know if I mess this up it's all on me not you. Glad to hear that because when your crying 15-20 years from about how messed up your life and you would've done better staying with Victor.

Well whatever Donna, James is here Victor is all the way in Daytona Beach Fl; a girl like me has needs. Like I said its gonna hurt Victor if you do this to him. Yes it will I'm gonna have to deal with this the rest of my life if I do it. Night girl just remember what I said and if you decide to go fourth with this then. Good night Donna I'll give you a call when I get out of work tomorrow. God what's my problem? I have a man that truly loves me with all his heart and has expressed it on more than one occasion. Then on the other hand it's this cute Irish fellow that's here and wants my affection all the time.

I'm scared God because if I decide to be with the other guy I might just lose Victor for good but then again how do I really know he's not down there chasing all those girls down there because we both know how much of a pussy hound he is God. Good night God I'll talk to you tomorrow morning when I get up. Hey stranger! How you doin James? I'm fine! So Rhonda what's it gonna be that nigga or me? Wow dude, let's get one thing straight if you're going to be with me you will refrain from that type of talk do you hear me? I wasn't raised that way nor will I allow anyone to have that talk around, nor fucked up karma.

Yes Rhonda! I thought it was okay because you decided to hang with me instead waiting for him. This is by chose and don't you ever forget. Victor will always be in my life regardless of what goes on between us. If I decide to be down with you I promise you this as long as I'm with you that you'll never have to worry about me messing with him in any sexual way but the first time I feel your abusing me, verbally or physically, and God forbid you cheat you'll never get this pussy ever again nor will you have a chance of living because I will contact Victor and he'll handle your fucking ass.

Rhonda I won't do that to you, I really like hanging with you and really can't wait to sleep with you once you get all that nigger juice out your system. Okay motherfucker, that's strike 2 if you get to 3 trust and believe you won't ever have the experience of even smelling a fart. James I gotta get ready for bed because I'm starting a new job with the Federal Government. Oh ya doing what? Working for SSA. That's golden I can't wait to see you. By the way a couple of my boys and I are going to City Mills Middle School to play 5 on 5.

Boy you don't want any of this I can play like a dude but still be dainty like a lady. Then I'm gonna have to see how great your game is. Good night! Good night to you too! Life is great right about now because I got a good job and two men that want this sweet Italian & Greek babe like me. I wonder if Victor made it to school okay?

Ain't this about to be some shit here I'm worried about the one man I want to break up with, I love him so damn much but this distance shit isn't gonna work not now. Maybe we can just take some time off from one another while he's away at school, I'll keep his pussy all tight and wet for him as well. I need to hear his voice right now before I go off to sleep and maybe he'll want to have phone sex with me? I'll page him right now. Damn that was quick! Hey babe! How was your trip? It was cool I got a place off campus this year because I have total custody of Dayna Maria!

Get out that's great so I'll have a place to stay when I come down to visit you? Yes baby, in fact I'll buy your ticket if you come down for homecoming. Yes yes yes! You know without a doubt I'll be down to visit you. Just make sure you get any of your other whores out before I get there. I will, baby but trust and believe I'm not cheating on you because not only do I want you to be my wife but also Dayna wants you to be her new mommy.

Really Victor! Yes that's all she's talked about since we left Waterbury 2 days ago. I'm so freaking excited right now, don't play with my emotions Victor because I can't handle this shit if you're lying to me. Rhonda I no about your trust issues as well as cheating on you, which I wont, do to you? Just don't screw me over Rhonda because if you do I wont ever forgive you nor will I want to be around you anymore. Babe if I'm not comfortable with being in our present situation I would be totally honest with you because I don't want to lose you as a friend you mean the world to me as well as my Little princess Dayna Maria, I'll love to be her mother and take her shopping for all those cute little girly shit.

Vic I gotta cut this call short because I start my new job in the morning. Get out you got the job with the Feds? Yes baby I did! I'm so proud of you I knew you were gonna get it when you applied for the job back in May when Dayna Maria and myself took you for the interview.

One last thing baby before we get off the phone can you talk dirty to me because my pussy is throbbing like a mutha. Okay if you want I gotta go into my living room because Dayna is sleeping in my room because I didn't get a bed for her yet. Okay! So Rhonda we're lying in our bed I'm stroking your hair as you lightly kiss my chest. Ummmm that's sounds good baby, what else? As your kissing my chest I begin to play with your lips I'm feeling your moisture from your lips. You whisper in my ear. Vic please grab my ass! I love when you grab my ass. I wanna suck your big juicy cock.

Damn Rhonda you're jumping the gun because I'm not even there yet. Baby all that talking your doing has my lady throbbing like you wouldn't believe. I wanna taste that sweet juice you shoot out of your love tool. Well tell me what you're doing right now. Well Vic I have my hands on my nipples pulling them and when you left Donna and I went to this place called LUV in Hartford for some sex toys. I bought one I call him Victor because it's light skinned like yours and just as thick as yours is.

So what are you doing with it right now? I'm playing with my clit and I have it on low so the pulsating will last longer for me. Ummmm Hmmmm. Yes Vic just like that baby you no what I want baby. Wow Gram and G Pa were some straight freaks. I can't believe how much stuff they did and waited that long to be married. Well remember I read just about all of her notebooks she had and there's a shocker in the about the 3rd or 4th one. I'm not gonna tell but you wont believe your eyes when you read it.

Raven what's in those books that more shocking then this? Just put it this way our aunt Robyn well that's all I got to say about that. Nah that can't be! Damn it, look at her and look at Auntie

Bree and Uncle Jimmy? You never paid attention how she looks a lot like my mother and your auntie. We've seen similarities in them but it never crossed our mind. I just thought she took on the Italian and Greek characteristics. Nah she took on her real father's characteristics. That also explains how much she hated James Simpson's Sr. she knew that bastard wasn't her father.

Well let's finish reading these books because if that's written down I wonder what other little secrets this family has? I can tell you this that Auntie Robyn's thing isn't the only secret they both went to the grave with. Oh shit this is gonna be a damn good book V3? Yes it is I just wish that G Pa wrote more about his part then what we found in his studio? Look I think we can join the both of them together at some point to show how much they loved one another over the years. That's why we need to stay with the title of Our Love because the more I read theses books I see it's all about Our Love.

Yes it was and is. Damn your right about that one V3 maybe we can break it down to sections from James Simpson to Victor Martin Sr. okay that will work as well. Now where was I in this story? You were at the part when she and G Pa conversation on the phone and having phone sex. Yep they sure were. Vic I wish I could smell you right now and have your breath in my nostrils. Damn Rhonda you miss me like that? Yes baby I don't know what I'm gonna do theses next few weeks before I see you babe.

Rhonda just promise me that you don't give up any of my sweet love until you see me.

Now you no I'm not a hoe. Yes but I thought by now you would've told me about this guy James Simpson that folks have been saying your talking to. What are you talking about Victor; I'm not cheating on you babe? Rhonda I don't give a shit if you are or aren't? Just tell me the truth because I need this from you I wont be mad nor will I hate you. Regardless of what happens between us babe I'm always gonna be there for you. Okay Victor I'll come clean with you, yes there is someone else his name is James Simpson I met him shortly after you got back home during summer.

We talked a few times and even went out on a couple of dates. He asked me out just before you left to leave to go back to school. What the fuck Rhonda? Really your gonna trade me in like that? Nah I'm scared to get tied down with one man, I've only been with 3 guys since I started dating. I've only slept with one of them and that was you. So your always gonna be special in my heart regardless. Rhonda oh Rhonda I want you but I don't know what to do because I'm 1269 miles from you now and I know you need sex on a regular after all of our rendezvous. You can trust me I wont do that to you until at least we see one another another in October.

Okay well good luck with your new job in the morning, I just want to let you no that I'm upset with you and I can forgive you. I will always be your baby as long as you tell me the truth I won't ever leave you baby even if the two of you get married to one another. Thanks Victor that's all I ask of you. I'm sorry I hurt you but like you said regardless what comes out of all this I'll always have a special place for you in my heart as well as my soul. Victor I love you babe. I love you too Rhonda. Damn G Pa had it like that? What do you mean Raven? Even though she was messing around on him she still knew her daddy was. Yep! I came across this in one of G Pa's journals a few years back I guess it was around the time they reconnected or so because it was straight Mack-Daddy or Iceberg Slim shit.

Really let us see it, maybe we can incorporate it into Our Love. Okay hold on I'm gonna go downstairs and grab it. Oh if y'all didn't get to this in her journal, did y'all know that Auntie Robyn isn't James's daughter? Hold the damn phone. What in the hell are talking about Raven? Robyn isn't James's she is. I'm telling you she isn't and he knew it from day one because he was told but they never said anything to his family either. So who's the dad then? Really you dumb ass sucka you can't figure that one out.

Nah! Yep! Holy shit so they we're still doing the do after both of them got married? Yep! Damn I need to hear more about that but go and get that stuff you wanted us to read Raven. I can't believe that one Dayvon. Well if it's true my mommy will know because they always talked to Dayna and she would know. Mom can you come here for a minute we got a question to ask you. Yes, what is it? Okay I don't know how to ask you this but Raven just told us that Auntie Robyn's biological father was G Pa, is that the truth? Yes he was and Robyn has known it every since she was about 13 or 14 years of age when she started noticing that she didn't favor any of her cousins on her father's side and her hair changed from that silky white folks hair to the nigga naps she's had ever since.

Well I'll be damn, that's straight gangsta. Well guys the story even gets better when she graduated from high school she carried a full load as well as working a part-time job and lettering in two sports, she had a 4.3 G.P.A. My daddy always told her that if she graduated with honors he would personally give her a check for $5000.00 in which he did but when she had her graduation party Rhonda invited him as well as Gabi they came but before leaving he handed her a set of car keys.

Now this is when I believe the abuse started with James and Rhonda or it was more known because it wasn't soon after that is when she had enough of all of his shit. So what kinda of car did he get her? C'mon you knew your G Pa and how he rolled. But he bought her a Grey Lincoln MKX. It was fly as hell. Damn like I said before he was straight Iceberg Slim or Pimp Daddy tip. Yep that was my daddy and I love him for that. Hey guys I'm back, now check this out who wants to read it first. What did y'all find of my parents now? Auntie Dayna I was downstairs in the studio with V3, my dad and I came across this and wanted to share it with them do you want to read it as well?

Yes I would love to read it as well. 1st off Mrs. Simpson, I contemplated all day yesterday how to say this to you as well as saying something positive you could live by also to make you smile as well. So here it goes, over the past year we fought, we argued, and laughed but through it all I knew I could depend on you, I shared things with you that I normally wouldn't. Then the icing on the cake was your inspiration for my breakout album. Victor may never get the chance to have Rhonda, but the love expressed over those 15 tracks is everything that I wish I could show you.

In closing you're a wonderful friend, beautiful person, and a phenomenal mother, a loyal daughter. Stay strong, be positive, and never give up because I will never turn my back nor give up on you. Damn my daddy was the truth. He knew all the right things to say to a woman. Its not ironic neither that they did eventually ended up together. Mom I saw a tear come down your face when you were reading it why? Well that's all I have left of either of the two mothers that cared for me, and the one man that never lied to me nor hurt me in any kind of way.

Mommy you were truly blessed, you had two strong women that showed you how to handle life and a man that exemplified love, power, health, and most important family. If he liked you he would go out of his way to do whatever but if rubbed him wrong or did anything to anyone he loved all hell was gonna break loose and he didn't stop until he broke you completely down. Yep that was my G Pa. now getting back to this other stuff with auntie Robyn. What else can we say about it? I'm just shocked that they we're still like that after they both were married to others.

Shit look at how happy they were together, did you ever not see them without a smile on their faces when they were around each other or just the mention of their name. Yes I always thought that was sexy as hell. Hey guys what are y'all in here talking about, I bet the family secret right? How did you no auntie? C'mon when we all get together like this the only thing we do is sit around and gossip or eat. But this isn't gossip it's the truth.

Yes it is I loved my mothers and father more than y'all will ever know. Then why did you give her so much hell then auntie? I wanted her to leave that son of a bitch that overly abusive to me. I learned at an early age that men could be very hurtful as well as evil. He would do things like pinch me; he even put a lit cigar out on my thigh and dared me to tell my mom. Wow Robyn I didn't no it was that bad between the two of you. I was so happy when I was 13 I think mommy and I were out shopping at the Buckland Hills Mall.

This very attractive man came over and grabbed her from behind and kissed her cheek before mommy could say anything. I thought mommy was going to kick this guy's ass but she turned around and said hey baby how are you doing. I was like what the hell mommy knows this sexy ass old man. She then introduced me to him, as this is Victor R. Martin Sr. It's a pleasure to meet you sir. I'm an ole friend of your mother's.

Okay I was wondering who you were grabbing my mother like that? So what brings you up here Mr. Martin? I'm just out looking for my fix. Your punk ass still buying shoes like a bitch. Rhonda that's not nice to say in front of our daughter like that. What in the world is that man talking about? Well baby we didn't plan to meet up like this it was by coincidence for us to run into one another like this. So stop beating around the bush please and answer question please. Victor did you eat yet? No I didn't, why you treating? Funny Victor, you got more ends then I would ever have. Okay I'll pay then. But, but wait mommy what the hell is this guy talking about? Baby we will sit down with you at dinner to tell you what this is all about.
Are you sure you want to do this Rhonda? Yes Victor everyday I look at her I think about how I wish my other children were by

you. Baby I told you that I wanted your sperm in me all the time. Um remember she's standing right here. Yes mom I am and I'm not naive as you may think mommy. Well okay baby I'm sorry I said those things in front you. It's not a problem at but if I think what it is your about to tell me that Mr. Martin is my father I kinda of figured that out on my own. How is that Robyn? Well Mr. Martin I favor my mother's side of the family a whole lot, but when it comes to that other person I look nothing like those pale face folks.

I also had a feeling about 3 or 4 years ago when my mommy was pregnant with my baby brother Jimmy. We all were on our way to see her in the hospital when this person I thought was my father came out and said to me that I could keep my nigger ass home because that baby boy isn't your brother at all. I was so hurt at what he said I called my Nana and told her what he had said to me. She called him and ripped him a new asshole. But Nana didn't say yea or nah about that if it was true or not. Can you just wait a few more minutes Robyn and your mother and I will explain everything.

Yes I can! Rhonda come over here for a minute I have something to ask you? Sure! What's wrong babe? Nothing I can't believe that we're finally coming out to let her know the truth? Victor Roosevelt Martin, I told you from the time I found out that I was pregnant with your daughter that she was gonna bring us back together and you laughed it off. I knew that this day was coming, now that she's gonna know the truth I want her to get to know her half-brother and sisters. No doubt Rhonda! She will get to know them as well as her cousins and biological grandparents.

What about Gabi? Ya what about her? Remember we don't have the best relationship going? She's always thought that you and I were fucking all along and this coming out she's gonna kill you or possibly me? Nah it aint even like that I'll have to easy into that anyway. Why do you say that Vic? Well you see the real reason why I'm up here is because she's in the hospital they found cancer in her cervix. Oh my God I'm sorry Victor is there anything I can do for you or the kids and I don't mean ass either?

Rhonda be there for me if I need a shoulder to cry on. Babe you already know I'll be there for you. Do you want a hug? Rhonda if you're giving them out I won't say no to it? Everything is gonna workout for the both of you just give it to God and he'll fix it for y'all. Rhonda I've prayed, I've cried, I even asked God to forgive me for having the affair with you just to make her healthy again. Babe I'm glad that you have that type of conviction in your heart, but remember it just wasn't you that knew what we were doing was wrong I too knew the consequences of fucking and sucking your cock unprotected.

Rhonda you didn't have to say it like that though. It's the truth that's exactly what I was doing to you for over 7 months, it only takes one time babe, and in fact I knew the exact moment that I conceived your daughter. Ya I kinda of knew to that time. I was happy on the inside I thought for sure you were gonna leave him for me? Damn that I knew I had you then I was just waiting for you to say the words Rhonda come live with me but that day never came. So I had to go around lying to folks saying that James and I are pregnant?

What a bold face lie I was telling to everyone. Our table is ready mommy and Mr. Martin. Okay Bree Bell we're coming. Wait how do you know my nickname? Who do you think give your mother the nickname many years ago? Dang mommy y'all got down like that? Martin table of 3 sir! Yes please follow me will you be interested in hearing our specials for today? Um that would be nice of you. We have blacken' catfish with sautéed fresh green beans and brown rice, center cut porter house steak, with a vegetable medley and pasta, last of all eggplant lasagna. Thank you! Can you give us a few minutes to decide?

Yes! Can I start you off with something to drink? I'll have a double of cognac. A for you ma'am can I have an apple martini. What can I get young lady? Do you have sweetened tea? Yes we do! I'll have that then sir. Okay Robyn I'm your father please don't be mad at your mom nor myself for keeping this secret away from you for all theses years. You can be as frank as you want as well as anything that you want to. Can I call you dad? Yes I'm more than happy to hear you want to call me that.

Okay! Now here's the personal stuff and please be honest because remember I'm already here. Why did you cheat on Jimmy, why didn't you save my mom from the hatred that he's put her through all theses years, and last of all are you guys still in love and if so what are you gonna do about it? Daddy I want you to start first. Robyn your mother and I have been in love with one another for the past 16 years, yes I'm still in love with your mother there's not a day that goes by that I don't think about her.

Robyn yes I wanted to save your mother but the timing wasn't never right. She's always known that I would be her savior from all his pain that he inflicted on her. Yes Robyn, Victor Martin Sr. is my one and only love I let him get away from me because I thought I was in love with James, it might have been true if he didn't feel the need to use me as a punching bag. I never felt unloved when I was around Victor never once raised a hand at me in hate nor pain. Baby as far as him not saving me is a tricky answer, because if he knew everything that was going in our house I would lose him as well because he would be on death roll.

Yes that is true my love bug; daddy would be sitting on death roll somewhere if she told everything. Your answers truly have touched me guys. Thanks Bree! Now I want to also say this I haven't said this to your mother since we we're dating in high school. What is that Victor? Rhonda if ever you need me in any kinda of way I'm saying this in front of our daughter don't hesitate to call me I'll come. If you need a shoulder to cry I'll be there, if you need a chest to punch my chest is there for that.

Awww my real dad is a hopeless romantic. Yes he is and has always been that way Robyn. So do I have any brothers and sisters daddy? Yes you do you have 2 sisters and 1 brother. Their ages are 24,19,15 in fact you look just like your sister Dayna who's just like you half African-American and Italian. Cool, but wait daddy your only 41 how is that you have a 24 year old daughter and still be involved with mommy. I was dating someone else before I met your mom she too was Italian. But unlike your mom she just wanted a half-breed child.

When your mom and I were dating back in our teens and my early twenties we took her everywhere? Then I went back to college she met James Simpson it was all over. So you mean to tell me that we all could've been Martin's and you would've been a happy woman. Yes, yes, yes, I'm telling you right now in front of your father that was one of my biggest mistakes I ever made in my life. The gut feeling never went away the whole time I've been with James.

Holy crap Auntie Robyn is all this true that we're reading in this journal? Yes it is, my parents were in love like you wouldn't believe it took Gabi's cancer and death as well as that asshole James's ass going to prison to bring them back together again. When she came to me and told me that they we're getting married I was overjoyed. So mom how was it being around Jimmy after you found out Victor was your real dad. I guess it was almost automatic that he really changed overnight. Like how mom and auntie? I was the little black monkey child, a pickaninny, and porch monkey.

Damn it I wouldn't allow no damn man talk to me that way I don't care if he was or wasn't my parent. It still hurts my soul to this day because of his hate he inflicted upon us meaning mommy and myself. Really! I bet it did auntie. There's more in the journal that mommy never shared with any of the kids. Well let's continue reading them. God I can't believe I've been with this man now for about 3 years I'm not happy at all I wonder what Vic is up too.

I bet my little Dayna is getting so big now? I need to stop thinking about him so damn much because I messed that up with him when I chose him over Victor. Hey Rhonda you have a visitor. Who is it Marvin? I don't know but he's rather charming. I'll be right there. Oh my freaking gosh Victor. Who's this little one he's a cutie. My newborn son Victor Jr. damn I guess it's over then for me ever getting you back Vic? Ya right like you would leave him for me? You never know babe. So how may I help you today? I need his social security card. So Victor I take it you found somebody because you had done had another kid on me.

Well when I came back home you just blew me away because you're happy with the white boy. Stop it Victor I don't see color but I see the inner person. Well if it ever gets to the point that you're not happy I'll still be there for you. I know this Victor more than you'll ever know. In fact if you had the balls to ask me out I might just be yours forever. Bullshit I doubt that but if you say so. Trust if you did my life would be totally different then what it is right now. Like what, I thought y'all were so damn in love.

The time I talked to Donna she was all like they just got back from Bristol Va., for some nascar race. Really that's some hillbilly shit. But not cutting on what he likes to do, we never did stuff like. I took you to cultural things as well as fun things with Dayna. Speaking of the little princess how is she doing is that bitch screwing with you? Yes as always even more now that I have full custody. Victor here's my number and address I live by myself so you can come over anytime you want. Now that's not a good thing because if we start back up doing anything I don't want him around anymore he doesn't treat you right and I know this.

How do you know this? Who's been running their fucking mouth like that? I'll tell you this no one has said anything bad about the two of you but judging by your reaction I can tell that your love is not true with him. So how's this baby mom, do I need to kick her freaking ass or you? Nah she gave me hell at first but she's different than what I dated in the past, she's got that fire like Kelli, the mouth of Mona, and the sex appeal like you. I bet she can't get it in like me? Well Rhonda that might be true, but I'm happy right now.

 Sure you are Victor, my skills made you feel like a natural man and I could put your ass to sleep like a baby when I was done as well. Rhonda stop it, so how's your man doing, I bet he can't do like I can. Babe just put it this way James isn't half of what you were to me. I haven't had a good nut off of a dick since August 8th 1993 our last time we were together. Ya those were the good ole days. But now I'm a dad times 2 so I'm defiantly off the market to women because I have two different babies moms.

Victor I wouldn't care if you had 8 different one's theses ladies know what there getting out of you a loyal, trustworthy, and confident mate. There's nothing sexier than that of a real man. I just wish I had listen to Donna. Well it was nice seeing you by the way here's my pager number Rhonda hit me up anytime. Remember I'll always be there for you regardless of your situation. Thanks that's great to know Vic and also that your not mad at me anymore. Your love is the one I lost.

I know I feel the same way I should've fought for you myself, but I didn't want to look like a stalker or whatever. Babe you weren't that nor did I ever feel that way around you. Hey remember I still love you Victor. I know baby someday! Ya when we're old and grey can't get it up that's when we'll be back together. Nah I'll have you before then trust and believe in that I will. There goes that strong Leo I grew to love. Yes it is! Bye Rhonda! Bye Vic can I have a hug before you leave?

Yes ma'am, tell your mom I said hello. I will it was nice seeing you. For rest of that day I was on cloud nine until I got home, that evening James was coming by with some of his friends that I became friends with as well for board game night. He arrived before everyone because he thought I was gonna give him some. Believe or not I was overly horny too because I saw the man I truly wanted to be with. So yes he could've got some, but the muthafucka came out of his mouth sideways which should've been a red flag but I took as him being jealous.

I told him that I had seen Victor and his newborn baby earlier in the day. Boy was that a dumb mistake he called me a fucking nigga lover, whore, and the word I truly hate cunt. I told him to leave that's when things went down hill; he swung at me just barely missing my face he kept on until he landed a punch in my stomach then to my face. I couldn't believe this was happening to me, what did I do to deserve this anger and beating I was getting.

I just told him I saw my ex-boyfriend and that was all. How am I gonna have breakfast with my dad in the morning with theses marks on my face? He's gonna want to kill him, and if I tell Victor what happened he's defiantly gonna die tonight. He finally left after about an hour or so of beating me and verbally abusing me. The first person I called was my mommy. She knew something was wrong as soon as she heard my voice that mother instinct kicked in, wanting to know what had happen. Once I had told her what had happened y'all knew my mother and that Greek blood got to boil.

She asked me if I called Victor to let him know what had happened. I laughed! She asked why was I laughing? I told her that's why we were fighting; I simply told him that I had seen Victor at my job today with his newborn baby. Damn I'm sorry you had to see the man you loved with another baby. Mom it's okay because if it's meant to be God will bring Victor back into our lives when he sees fit. I'm just scared because I'm going to breakfast with daddy in the morning if he sees me like this I'm afraid of what he might do to him.

Well baby all I can say I dated your dad and was married to him he wasn't a hitter he just couldn't keep his dick in his pants. I know this mommy, but remember I'm daddies little girl so he'll probably end up killing him. Listen ease your dad into it in fact have him come over your house so you have the upper hand. Would you like for me to come over? Mommy yes maybe the three of us can game plan on what to do? I guess. Well I'm gonna go lay down I'll see you in the morning. Okay baby love you.

Love you to mommy, I forgot to tell you that my baby told me to tell you hello. See that's a nice young man, I wish he was still around I love his manners and his thoughtfulness. Someday mommy we'll be back together again. Baby only God knows the answer to that one. Yes night! Goodnight baby. Where did I put his number? I wonder if he would come over if I page him? Here it is! Hello did someone page me from this number?

Yes silly it's me! Me who? So I stop talking to you, sleeping with you, moaning your name really. It's Bree Bell! What's wrong, I didn't think I would hear from you this soon. I need you, come over please. What's wrong babe? Nothing just come over. I'll be over in a few to see you. Okay I'll leave the door open also your not going home tonight either. Damn this must be serious Rhonda.

Yes it is, I'll see you in a little bit right? Promise me that you'll come! Rhonda I'm coming now I should be there in a couple minutes so. Okay like I said I'll leave the door open for you just come in and sit down I'm jumping in the shower right now and don't you try anything either because I can still beat that ass Vic. I wont but I'm really curious why you want me to come by is everything okay. Yes Victor I just want your company for the night is that okay with you? Yes I'm okay with that Rhonda. Bye bye.

Yep see ya in a few. Alright when he gets here he's gonna go the fuck off when he see's my face, should I tell him what James did, if I tell him what he did Victor will end up in jail and I won't get the dick that I need so damn bad. Damn that was quick I didn't even get a chance to wash my ass yet. Oh well I guess he'll just have to take a shower with me then. Hello Rhonda! I'm here. Okay Victor, I'll be right down or you can come up to my bedroom if you want? Nah I'll wait or you to come downstairs.

Well when I come downstairs promise me you won't get upset when you see me. Why would I get mad at you Rhonda that's not me and you know that? Yes Vic I do I just don't want you angry or upset with me. Here I come, put on some music and I have some homemade wine that my dad made. Sounds good, did you eat yet? I order something for us. No I didn't, whatever you want to order I'm cool with it. Hey babe! What the fuck is wrong with your face, what did this? Remember I told you not to get angry with me. Yes I did say that to you. Now explain to me how this happen to you, did he do this to you Rhonda? Um well ahhhhhh, um! Damnit stop beating around the bush and tell me the truth.

Hold me please Victor. Yes come here lay your head on my shoulder and tell me everything. Well he came over after work because we were gonna play some board games with some of his friends I was excited that I had seen you today with your newborn son speaking of which where is he at? He lives with his mother, now stop trying to get off subject.

Damn I hate that you know me so freaking well Vic. So I told him I had seen you at my job with your newborn son. So it was okay for a few seconds then it was like he was possessed by the devil. He started calling me a nigger lover, cunt and tried hitting me a couple times before he connected with my stomach and then my face. Okay I'm pissed but me fighting him isn't gonna solve anything me being in jail won't help at all baby. Go get your house phone and call the police. I don't want that to happen either Victor. So what your saying is you don't mind him beating you on a regular basis then?

No Victor not all I'm just scared if that happens that he will do it again but kill me. Well I'm here now I'm not going anywhere ever. If you say so Victor! Yes I do, now call them they'll help you and you can get a protection order against him. Thanks Victor I don't know what I would do if you weren't in my life anymore. Go wash your face I'll order our food and wait with you for the police to arrive. Your so damn sweet I wish I hadn't pushed you away or you should've fought harder for me.

By the way it's also your lucky night because you'll have the pleasure of making love to me. In fact from now on you can have it whenever you want. Rhonda I don't think that will be a good look. Why Victor? Because you know how we get down once we start we can't stop it. Vic I don't care because I want you, I'm telling you I messed up big time letting you get away the way I did.

Rhonda I understand completely, but I just had my son I'm in love with his mother. C'mon Victor your saying that you're not into this body anymore, my tits are soft and firm, my butt is big and round with side dimples, the pus is off the chain? Yes it is all that Rhonda, but how would you feel if you just had a baby and the father of that child just up and left you for another woman?

I would be hurt, I would want to kill that bitch, and cut his muthafuckin' balls off. So why would you want to do this then? Victor I love you, I've always felt that way about you.

Thanks for sharing babe. Here's something that we can tryout. What Victor? We can set up something where we can be with one another like 2 or 3 times out the year, also I'm not gonna wear any protection either so if you get pregnant what are you gonna do about it? Victor if you get my ass pregnant trust and believe we're keeping our baby. Okay what if your married to him, what are you gonna say when he or she comes out darker complexion than any of your other children? Victor that's a path we're gonna have to pass if and when it happens.

Okay I believe the police just pulled up. Can you go and check for me if so let them in as well? Yes babe I will. Hello thanks for coming. Is Ms. White home? Yes she is, we've been waiting for you. Might we ask who you are to the compliant? I'm a close friend she called me after she was attacked. Hello Ms. White I'm officer Hayes and this is officer Gilmore. Can you please explain to us what happened and we will tell you what course of action you can take?

Well sir and madam I came home excited today after a very trying day at work. One was that my man was coming over with some friends to play board games. Then look at him what female wouldn't be excited seeing that 6ft 4in tall man of color. I hope I'm not speaking out of place but I feel you on that one Ms. Yep! So when my boyfriend James came in the house he saw that I was in a good mood and asked me why? I told him that I had seen Victor and his newborn baby today at my office.

Damn its always the good ones that got somebody girl. Yes officer Hayes. I had explained to him that Victor had came into my office to get his sons social security card. So what happened after that he was cool then out of nowhere it was like he was possessed by the devil he swung at me, I was able to duck a couple of times then he connected with my stomach then my face. Not only did he physically abuse me he also verbally abused me.

I know I should've called y'all first but I called Mr. Martin he's always been my saving grace. Okay ma'am here's what's gonna happen tonight we're gonna issue a warrant for his arrest he'll be processed charged with 3rd degree assault and 2nd degree evading arrest. After all that he'll have a chance to bail himself out but there's no need to worry about him bothering you because there's also gonna be a protection order against him.

Is there anything else that you would like to share with us before we leave? No sir, I'm just glad that you were able to help me out with this problem. Ma'am if you feel there's anything else that you would like to add here's the number to our detective's office because they will be taking over for us. Thanks once again. Your welcome! Ms. White I do have to say woman to woman your friend is fine as hell I know what I would be doing with him if he were in my life. Well as soon as the two of you leave I will be getting it in with him. Baby I think our food is here as well, I'll go out and get it while you finish up with the officers.

Thanks sweetie. Excuse me ms can I ask you something really quick. Yes officer Hayes! Girl if you don't end up with him slide me his number because I could do damage with man. Nah I'm not gonna let him get away from me again. Well here's my business card if there's anything I or my partner can do for you feel free to give us a call. Thanks very much once again. Bye y'all.

Vic we can eat down here or in my bedroom. It's totally up to you but I believe if I make it up to your room you know I wont be eating food but something else. Well Vic since you put it that way I think I'm gonna opt out on dinner and let you taste that sweet nectar that I have between my legs. I don't want you to think that I invited you over here just to fuck me; I want you here to protect me because I'm scared. Why are you crying baby it's not a big thing? Yes it is

Victor because you don't understand why I need you? If that were the case my black ass would be here all the time my newborn son would be ours not my new girlfriend Gabi. So that's her name what does she look like? I bet she can't take all that in her ass or deep in her sweet women parts? Yes Rhonda she can but as far as the ass you know black women don't do Greek at all. I guess your gonna have to swing by here whenever you want some of that ass action. Like I said before it's a strong possibility of us keeping this going.

Okay Victor I'm so happy that you decided to come of all days to my job. I almost didn't come into work but something kept telling me to go. I don't know why but whenever I came around the corner and saw your fine ass standing there with that adorable baby I was like thank you God for making me come into work. Rhonda I almost didn't go myself I had a lot of running around to do and by chance I ended up at the post office I said to myself what the hell, I knew you were employed there but I wasn't sure if you were working today or not so I just asked the man at the front desk if you were in and to both of our surprise we're here right now laying across your bed watching 90210.

Yep and I'm about to rock your world as soon as I'm done with this steak and baked potato. I just can't believe that after all the shit I did you're here not judging or trying to hurt me even more than I am right now. Promises me this Victor that you'll be there for me forever, I don't care about your relationship with Gabi or mine with James I don't want us to ever be apart. I love you with all my heart if I could've turn the hands of time to that August night when you left to go back to school I would've listen to my mommy and Donna as well I guess hindsight is 20/20 an your not gonna be replaced by no one do you hear me?

Yes Rhonda, I'm so into you and have always been. I'm just scared of what might happen to you I don't feel safe in leaving you here when I leave in the morning? Victor I'll be okay as long as you and my father are in my life. Stop crying Rhonda! I promise I'll be there for you we just have to workout our particulars and everything will be fine. Vic can I do that special thing that you love so much. What is that Rhonda? You know silly, that bomb ass head I used to give you. Well it's good with me as long as you let me go down on you.

Now Victor you know you don't have ask me that my legs are always open for your tongue. Your so nasty Vic but I am totally down for your magic it's like fire and desire when you do that to me. So how are we gonna do this you wanna 69 or just straight go down on one another. Let's just see where it takes us babe. I'm down with that Rhonda, I gotta pee then I'll be ready for all of you. Okay Vic! Hey Dayven can you believe what we're reading here? Nah this is some amazing stuff here how the two of them went around portraying that they were just good friends. Bullshit Ravon! Theses guys were so full of shit. G Pa and Gram did all this stuff, now I'm wondering if karma showed it's ugly head throughout their relationship. What do you mean by that V3?

Well its simple because look at Gramma Gabi her cancer and death G Pa was upset but he had Gramma Rhonda in his back pocket, she knew he would be there for her regardless of what others might think of them. True but she had more freaking turmoil than him. Um she brought that upon herself having an outside child yes I'm saying that out loud my mommy was the bastard child but that kept they're bond so strong between them. Moms can you come here for a minute as well as you dad. Yes! What's wrong? Did y'all know about the family secret? Well I guess so daddy judging by the look on your face.

Yes we all knew about it by the time we got older because the older she got the more she would act just like the two of them. Did she, she had a lot of Victor's mannerisms would fly off the handle I can remember one time she was visiting G Pa and Gabi as well as babysitting for Dayna. Gabi had said something to her about her mother, I can't remember exactly what it was but she cussed out Gabi told her to goto hell because her mother cared more about Victor than she ever would, and that they were still having sex on a regular. The look on my mother's face was priceless.

She broke down crying you know how Vic would yell scream, go off, then the next minute calm as the wind. Yes! Well that's what exactly what she did, Gabi started to cry hysterically she said why are you crying Gabi? You're a fucking hateful child I can't believe you came from my husband? I'm dying of cancer and you would say something like this to me. If you were my child I would've kicked your ass all up and down this house. But I don't have the strength to do it. When your father gets home we're gonna have a long talk about respect and how you need to act around me understood.

Yes ma'am I understand you. Can I say this to you before my daddy gets home from work? Yes Robyn, what is it? I'm sorry for my behavior you have to see my point of view you're a wonderful person, but my biological father and mother aren't together I live with a man that verbally and mentally abuses me on a regular then I come over here and I see how you look at me with discuss I didn't ask to come into this world Gabi it happened 16 years ago it's not my fault neither is it yours but I'm apart of this family regardless if you want me to or not. When I come over here I feel the love and that's all a girl like me wants. I get it you see Dayna in me and wonder how many other women are out there with Victor R Martin Sr.'s kids.

Girl you hit that one on the head. I'm not mad at you at all I just see my husband fucking your mother when he should've been home doing that to me. I have gotten over the fact that happened 16 years ago but every time you come around I see it all over again. Well I don't mean for that to happen ma'am. You'll find out when you get older no matter what you do in life there's always gonna be some woman that wants to sleep with your man. Your father is home now.

Can we not have this discussion right now because I'm really trying my best to get to know my father; I wish y'all would just let me stay with you. At least here I would be loved and cared for by everyone at least. Hi daddy! Robyn I didn't know you were coming over today? Yes Dayna called me to see if I could babysit the twins for her, I told her yes. Well judging by the calmness in here the two of you are getting along as well Gabi? Um we had our words but we discussed something's and have decided to listen to one another. Okay! So where are my grandbabies at and what's for dinner? The twins are sleeping and I made reservations for us at Lenny & Joe's in New Haven. I love that spot. I know you do Victor we have to go over something's the doctor had discussed with me.

There's also going to be a visitor with us. Who is Gabi, what are trying to do? Nothing baby I just have to get some shit off of my shoulders. Okay! What time are we eating dinner? I told our guest to meet us there around 7:30. So I have time to wish my ass. Yes you do Victor. Daddy can I talk you before you take your shower? Yes! What's up Bree Bell? Daddy I'm afraid for mommy and I. why is that has he harmed you or your mother in any kind of way? His verbal abuse is out of control, he's always calling mommy a nigger-loving whore, and me the black tar baby.

Hold up the last time I talked to her she said everything was okay. Daddy she's always going to tell you that because her stubborn Italian and Greek ass is scared that you will kill him. She needs you, I need you, and most of all Gabi needs you. Yes I know this, Bree Bell I want the best for your whole family except for that piece of shit she's married too. Daddy I think it's honorable that you'll still fight for mommy even though the two of you physically have been with one another for many years. Thanks for the heads up baby girl. Gabi do I hear our grandbabies? Yes they're up but don't go messing with them just yet.

Why not I gotta spoil my babies while their still young? If you spoil them anymore than what you're doing now I would hate to see once they get older. Gabi like you don't do the same, your forever taking them shopping buying them everything under the sun. Yes I'm guilty of that but what get's me is why does she have to buy them stuff as well? Well it's simple she's been in

Dayna's life since she was one and a half years old. She might have even been her stepmother.

Wow muthafucka, it's okay for your 2 outside daughters to come into my house but I'll be damn if you come out your mouth and say some shit like that. I didn't mean anything by it. You knew about Dayna I never hid Dayna from you on the other hand Robyn wasn't a mistake we we're in a bad place at that time as well as Rhonda and him I've always been there for her so when it happened I just knew that it would lead to a divorce. We didn't get one nor did she. Life is too short to keep bring this shit up. If you want out then just say the word we can go on our own separate ways. No I don't want that at all, in fact I've come to the conclusion that as long as the two of you are alive that I'm gonna have to deal with you guys fucking around rather it be sex or just hanging.

I get that but if you're so damn uncomfortable with her and me I'll leave. Shut the fuck up Victor and get your ass in the shower so we can get ready to leave for dinner. Hey mommy I'm going out tonight do you mind watching Bree and Jimmy? Where are you going tonight? Get this I'm meeting up with Gabi and Victor at Lenny & Joe's in New Haven. Are you sure about that baby what if she goes off and kills the both of you? Yes mommy, she's the one that asked for this so I'm guessing maybe she's ready to call it quits so I can finally get Victor.

Girl you're still married to that monster, he would kill all of us if you left him. Mommy I'm not scared of either one of them because I know Victor has my back. What time is Robyn coming home tonight or is she spending the night at her dad's house? I'm not sure mom but I believe she's watching Dayna's twins, I can text her if you want me too? Yes please do! What time will he be home tonight if he's coming home? Mom to be honest with you I don't give a rats ass what time he does, I'm so done with the abuse and the lying. So why don't you do something about it then?

I wish I could but I can't do all this on my own, granted Vic helps out but I don't want him thinking he's gotta help me out of situations all the time. Well we know how he's been to the both of us for the past 17 years now. Yes he's great but it's time I did for me mommy. Just pray on it girl and see where God leads you too? Yes ma'am I'm getting ready to go now how do I look? Like a million dollars baby! You're just saying that because I'm your daughter though. Yes you are but I have no reason to lie to you either.

Okay I'm out! Rhonda do not think anything crazy out of this. I don't understand why I talk to myself but I know this if I have my way one of theses days he's gonna be mine. God forgive me for wanting another woman's man but if he wasn't suppose to be around you would've made it so. But who am I to question you

God I'm just a jezebel who has slept with a married man. My heart cries out for your forgiveness I just wished I had done the right thing years ago when I got pregnant with our beautiful daughter that you blessed us with. Let me give Donna a call to see what she's up to?

Hey gurl how are? I'm gravy what are you up to? I'm on my way to meet up with Victor and his wife. What the hell? Yes you heard me Donna correctly. I'm just shocked that you're meeting up with them. I was even more shocked that she called me. So what do you think this is all about? Your guess is as good as mine. Maybe she's gonna grant Victor his divorce. Girl your stupid you know damn well she's not gonna do that at all. Stranger things have happened Rhonda.

Yes that's true, but I'm not getting why all of this, I'm kinda of nervous to see what this is all about. Girl! Give me a call when you're done with your evening. I will Donna! Where are y'all meeting up? Lenny & Joe's in New Haven! Damn I guess their pulling out all the punches for this one. Yes they are well I'm almost there now I'll hit you up when I'm done. Okay please do.

Alright Rhonda get your game face on and whatever happens tonight I'm gonna be strong I don't know if this is necessary or even relevant to your meet with the Martin's, just try to go into all of this with an open heart because I think this is something that everyone will walk away feeling great. If you say so girl, I just pulled up here but I don't see any of his vehicles out here though. Are you sure they said Lenny & Joe's Rhonda? Yes damn it! Okay no need to get ugly about it Rhonda. I'm not being ugly; I just want to know what the hell this is all about girl. I think I see them now, what the hell when did he get that? What are you talking about Rhonda? Victor and Gabi just got out of a grape colored XK8.

Girl where have you've been he's had that for a minute now. When the fuck did you see him driving that, I'm the one he's got a baby by and we screw on a regular I haven't seen nor heard about this car. Ya your right on that Rhonda don't make a seen though. I won't at all; I'm out for now I'll hit you up when I leave. Okay girl! Is it me guys or did she spend a lot of time on her relationship with G Pa than James? Nah she talks a lot about James throughout all of her journals.

She really loved him but he was such a lose cannon that she was scared for her life; he forced her back into Victor's arms forever. So is there any of that info in any of theses journals about that? Yes once we finish this particular entry she really gets into the whole love affair with James. Then how much longer do we have to wait to see it? If I'm not mistaken guys right after this one here Gram goes into detail about meeting and dating him. Cool I can't wait to see what she has to say about this guy. Ya I know! Then lets get back to entry then. I'm for that! Hello Victor & Gabi! How are the two of you doing this evening? We're blessed and highly favored.

I hear that! So can I ask you Gabi why you asked for me to meet with you and Victor here tonight? Yes you can! I know the two of you are still sleeping with one another so please don't lie to me about that off the bat. As much as it hurts me I've learned to deal with that, but what hurts my heart deeply is the fact that I'm going through this ovarian cancer thing by myself. He should be here caring for me not running to your rescue every time you know what never mind. No Gabi say what's on your mind and since we're speaking this way I want to be very frank with you. Okay every time that piece of shit husband puts his hands on you or you feel scared about something you call my husband away from his family.

It's bad enough I have to look at your 16 year old mistake. But when that happens it fucking pisses me off like you wouldn't believe. Well Gabi first of all I'm very sorry that your going through all that pain, second of all whenever I call him the first thing I ask him is it okay for him to leave. I'm already on the bad side of the fence I don't want to mess up or fuck up anything else. So why do you have to have my man as well Rhonda? He's a caring person sexy as hell and wonderful in bed I get that, but why my man Rhonda why? Gabi I never went into this to take him away from you in fact I feel like you've stole him away from me Gabi.

Bitch please I didn't take him away from you Victor told me everything so I believe its been mutual on both sides why the two of you have been doing this for so long. I get it he saved you he did the same for me he made me feel like a woman again. But I'm gonna tell you this just like he's been screwing you behind my back and in front of me as well he's gonna do the same to you when y'all get together. Hey what do you mean when we get together Gabi?

Victor I invited her here to let the both of you know that it's comeback even stronger than the last time all that damn chemotherapy isn't working this time the doctor's have given me 6months to a year to live. The only one that knew about all this was my baby Dayna! Now lets wait one minute, Dayna is my love bug she's kept a secret from her dad. Yes Victor I told her not to say anything to you because I knew what was going on at Rhonda's because Robyn and I talk all the time when she's over the house.

Yes we know this she shares with me all the time how she has the best of both worlds having two loving mothers that care for her and a father that's out of this world. That is all true Gabi and Rhonda she is truly loved by all that are here, but as far as you calling her a mistake she wasn't we both knew what we we're doing from that first nut up until the time she came into this earth. I'm just mad she had to endure the turmoil all of those years before she found out the truth.

Yes why the hell did y'all hide it from her for 14 years or better yet let that lie go on for 14 years a blind ass Ray Charles could've seen all through that bullshit. Don't blame me Gabi that was all Rhonda. Yes it was all me I didn't want people to judge me for having sex with a black man but anyone that's ever known me knows that's what I preferred and the fact that I got pregnant by my ex boyfriend was the way it was suppose to happen.

Well I'm getting totally off subject were I wanted this conversation to go. Okay sorry Gabi, please finish. Well like I was saying before the doctors are only giving me a short time to live I want you to take care of my husband. Since I've had to share him with you after all theses years. I wouldn't want any other woman to be around my children and grandchildren I know they will be truly loved by you and Victor just make this promise to me that you divorce that man before he kills you or your mother. He's no good for you at all; I see the fear in your eyes whenever you speak of him.

Girl you should be walking around here with an opened eye not with your eyes closed better yet showing how our loved prevailed through everything. Yes Gabi I know all that is true, but he's broken me down so much that I even second guess things when Victor does it for me. I have had a wall that was up and he's broken it down for me that I can trust and also believe in myself as well as a man I've loved for many years.

Girl sometimes its like that I understand everything now I know why God has this in my destiny, I hated you with a passion Rhonda how you could get Victor to do whatever you needed him to do but gave me major attitude when I would ask him to do the same for me. I would be like what does this fucking white cunt got that I don't? Well Gabi that's where your wrong because this asshole right here would do the same to me but I always threaten him with sex and how he wouldn't ever get it from me if he didn't do what I asked him to do.

Bullshit girl that doesn't work for me. Um obviously because he was coming to me for that! Is this true Victor and how often did you do this playing one of us for the other? Shit I was still doing that as early as this year. It works Gabi trust me when I say this to you. Right Victor? Yes Gabi, I'm so sorry that all this is happening to you, but I have great news for the both of you though. Ya what is it babe? Well I've been talking to Bob,

Lamone, Jay and Marion we're thinking about putting the band back together in fact I've written 3 songs so far.

Well that's great for you and the boys. But will you have time to do all this with everything going on with me? Yes Gabi, I think that now Rhonda and I know what's going on we'll both be here to help in any kinda of way. Well that will be wonderful not only are you saying to me that your gonna continue to be with her when I need you but I'm gonna have to endure her helping around the house? No Gabi I want to help you out, I'm not trying to steal your husband away from you we both love him equally I just want theses last couple of months that you have on this earth to be as enjoyable as possible.

That might be all well and good but I'm kinda of leery of it all. Now Rhonda why the hell are you crying? Nobody I mean nobody ever believes me, I'm tired of always being used and abused by everyone that's suppose to have my back. At this rate Victor and you too Gabi I don't want this nor do I need this bullshit in my life. Look the both of you need to shut the hell up right now, Gabi I get why you feel that way, on the other hand I also see where your coming from as well if I could just have someone like you in my corner that's going thru all this and can still be strong I could get away from James Simpson Sr. my kids are young though.

Bullshit girl Robyn is 16 going on 17 Bree is 14 and lil Jimmy is what like 9 or 10 now what would you rather have them see you constantly abused and possibly killed by the hands of that monster or be able to walk away with a fresh start. Yes I'm pissed that I have to share Victor with you but look at it this way at least you have a man that truly cares for you and will protect you from him. Gabi I don't want to hurt you or put you through anymore pain than what your already in.

Rhonda I think if Victor lost the both of us he wouldn't know what to do, look at him right now he's sitting across from the both of us thinking about it right now. Right Vic? To be honest with the both of you I've been thinking about that for along time I even put myself in the equation how would the two of you be able to carry on if I were to pass away. Knowing the both of you and how I impacted both of your lives it would be extremely hard on y'all.

Rhonda maybe 4 or 5 years then you would follow me to heaven, Gabi I would say maybe 2 or 3 years because of your medical problems and the bond we have. You might just be right on that Victor for the both of us. But answer our question to you? I would be lost but I would have to be strong for your mom Rhonda, then as far as the kids I would have to raise them as mine blend them in with my four, which would be extremely easy because they all know one another quite well. Can I get anything else for you this evening? No ma'am but I would like the bill please.

I would also like to say that your service was delightful. Thank you sir and madams, I try my best! Well we all thank you for being so attentive to us as well as everyone in your station. Thanks that means a lot. Your welcome! Victor you pay for the bill I'm gonna go and use the bathroom. Okay! I'll go with you Gabi. So Gabi what did you really want this meeting for? I'm a woman that's been in and out of your relationship every since you had VJ. I know this, I've learned to forgive every since this last bout of cancer that's been kicking my ass.

I stopped fighting with him and wishing ill will on you because what is that fixing nothing at all. Promises me this that you divorce that piece of shit husband your married too first, then make sure you never hurt Victor and the two of you continue your bond and let him help you because his heart is so true when he sets on something. I will Gabi, if you need me for anything don't hesitate to call me even if it's just to vent. Remember I just went through this cancer thing with my daddy and if it weren't for Victor and my mommy I would've lost it big time. I hear that, lets get out of here before he thinks we're in here trying to kill one another.

What the hell is this? What Rhonda? I just received a text message from James ranting about some bullshit. Are you all right? Yes I am! Well you can ride back to the dirty water with us. Thanks but I'm good, but if I have any problems I'm gonna contact the police this time around. Okay Rhonda I also know you wanted to say Victor as well? Yes I did but I didn't want to get you all upset. If need be call him okay Rhonda? Thank you. Rhonda I don't get you, I tell you I love you almost everyday, and there's not a day that goes by that I don't think about you. It seems like yesterday that we met.

Taking rides to look at trucks and doing stuff like that. Kissing in the movies, having our first child. Even though I found out that she wasn't I still tried to raise her, as mine even though I knew it was that nigger's baby.

The road has been bumpy I'm glad you stuck around and believe in me. So on the eve of our oh I mean you and that nigger bastard daughters birthday and the day I asked you to be my girlfriend I just want too let you know that I care about you and I love you. I hope I'll be able to spend another 50 years or more with you. James that was nice that you were able to come up with something like this but I think it's a few years to late, as far as you saying you love me I'm sorry to tell you that you've haven't said that to me in years.

Rhonda I know this seems like the only why I can talk to you without yelling or even hearing your input but it is the only way I can do this? I'm very sorry for hurting you earlier today. This is heartfelt; you're the only woman I've dealt with that has accepted me for me. But yet I feel the need to break you down with my words and hands.

 I know I could've said this to you when we we're talking, but me knowing you would've started with bullshit or something like that. For once in your life I want to take you seriously but I think it's to late because of your bond with porch monkey and his band of coons. I don't mean to hurt you but I'm sick and I thought going for help would fix things and I guess it isn't. I want to grow old and grey with you but at the rate I'm going that probably won't happen. You may not believe it but I do care about you, why else would I try controlling you and not allowing you to do anything that I don't agree with.

But you do it anyway that's the reason why I get so upset with you and strike you. But then I hurt when I do dumb shit to you and the kids. My heart is with you my mind is with you. It's just the fact that your giving my pussy away to that fucking tree swinging monkey is what hinders our relationship. I believe in you and the kids I just wish you could see that's why I beat you and treat the kids the way I do. My life is what it is. I'm the only one that can change it neither you nor anyone else.

You're a great woman and I see why he's crazy about you and your crazy for him. James there's one thing that you'll never have that Victor has? That is what bitch? Wow lets not talk about your mother like that. Shut it up before I beat you again Rhonda. That's what I'm talking about, you don't fucking get it at all. You say you want me, you say you love me, then you come out of your mouth with that. Victor has never said anything like that to me nor would he.

I bet he will once he gets to know the real you Rhonda. At first you were the same way with me screwing my brains out and other things then you became a straight bitch. Oh my god your really gonna go there? You forgot about the cheating and lying that you've been constantly doing from day one. Victor knows me way better than you he pays attention to me. I feel loved when I'm with him, I don't fear for my life like when I'm with you.

James you scare me, and the children. You proclaim that you love me but no one in his or her right mind would ever say that then say I gotta beat you to keep you in line. For that I have to say fuck you and the person that taught you those ideas is just as fucked up as you are. James you just don't know how much you meant to me. I dated you because I wanted too, I married you because I was in love with you, and I had your kids because I knew you would be a wonderful father. Boy was I fucking fooled by all of that.

No Rhonda you weren't fooled I was all that but you started talking to that nigger baboon better yet you never stopped talking to him. All theses years I thought Robyn was my daughter then when I found out that fucking tree-swinging nigger got you pregnant I raised her like she was mine. I hated you for that but I forgave you. Hold up James all the fucking you did, let's not forget about your Puerto Rican princess you've been sleeping with and got her pregnant the same time I was pregnant.

You can say whatever you want about Victor, his family, hell even our daughter Robyn, there's nothing like a man that will stick up for you regardless of life's situations. Yes I had perks a tall handsome black male with a big dick, and know how's to make the kids feel safe as well as I. Well if you feel that way Rhonda, how's he gonna feel when I kill you? Did you just threaten me? If I did what are you gonna do about it, it's my word against yours?

Your freaking girlfriend Donna and her fat ass boyfriend Bryan isn't gonna do shit and if you even think about bringing that nigger here I'll kill him as well. You know what James on that note I'm out, I'm so freaking done with you and the bullshit that you've put me through. This is the last straw when you said that shit about killing me. I want you gone when I get back do you hear me James? I don't want any bullshit out of you either; you can go back to Beacon Falls with the rest of your racist's family.

You can't stand here and say anything like that, that's why I never mind? That's why what James your big and bad finish your tirade because it looks like you gotta get some shit of your chest. Bitch please if I gotta move out and you decide you want to divorce me it's not gonna be peaceful for you or him. James do what you have to do because I'm gonna protect my family. If I find out you've done anything fucked up or did anything to ruin my credit. Boy God help you if you did.

Mommy please calls the police for me as well as Victor. Is everything okay Rhonda? I want him out I'm done he needs to leave now. I'm gonna go outside to calm down because if I stay here any longer I think something really bad is gonna happen. Rhonda I will, but it's not gonna pretty if you get the cops involved. Mommy I need protection for us. Baby I understand this, but he's freaking crazy I could see him coming back here setting this house on fire. Do you think he's capable of doing something like that? Yes Rhonda! He fucking threatened your life and the kids.

If you don't do it I'll do it? This asshole better be glad your
father passed away last year. Mommy I don't want that either,
Victor is gonna go crazy when he hears everything I've been
dealing with. Yes he will, but knowing Vic he's gonna help you
through all of this bullshit. My question to you Rhonda is why
did you stick around all theses years? Don't give me that bullshit
about the kids; I left your father when you were young and look
how you turned out.

I raised you along with your father and I know damn well he
wouldn't want you to go through all this strife. Mom I'm seeing
it now Victor is helping me to see through all this. I'm just
scared that I won't be as strong as you were. Come here, and
give your mother a hug. Your support system is bigger than you
think. Do you think so mommy? Yes baby I know so. Nana
Helen why is mommy crying? Lil jimmy your mom and dad had
a disagreement.

I don't think that was an argument that I heard he threaten my
mommy and she's been crying ever since do something please
before he injures mommy again. I called the police and they're
on the way. I've been trying to get Victor but he's not answering
his phone. Nana I think I over heard Robyn talking to Calven
she said that Victor was following the ambulance Gabi had
taken a turn for the worse.

What? Yes nana she was unresponsive and some other stuff that I didn't understand. Oh my God this asshole here is hurting my daughter and Victor dealing with Gabi. God I hope that whatever you have planned for the two of them is soon I'm about ready to lose my damn mind. Boy I cant believe this guys G Pa and Gram surely went through a lot just to get to the life they had afterward. She was walking around with her Eyes Closed and he just wanted to Open her Eyes, so that they could share Our Love. Yes they did V3 but it seems like where getting to the good parts now.

You got that right Ravon so continue reading please. Hey Vic, how's Gabi doing? Rhonda it doesn't look good at all. Why? What happened? She's sicker than she lead us to believe when we went out to eat. Really! Yes Rhonda they're talking about doing surgery again to relieve some of the pain. Damn babe I'm sorry to hear that. Do you need anything from me? Just say a prayer for us please. Okay I'll do that.

 Um babe before you hang up can you tell me why your mom called my phone 3 times and didn't leave a message? I don't know baby. I hope your not lying to me Rhonda because I don't need that right about now. Well since your gonna be my husband someday, I cant lie to you Victor. Then just tell me what's up then? Well when I got home tonight after hanging out with some friends he accused me of sleeping with you and threaten to kill the kids and me.

Wait a muthafuckin minute are you serious babe? Yes I am that's why mommy was calling you so much. Are you okay now? Yes I am I had to go in on him about his little Spanish whore he's been screwing for years Kelli Quinoas. Last Thursday night Donna was out with some of her co-workers at Pizza Castle when she saw him and her out. She went over to speak to him but he didn't acknowledge her.

So Donna gave me a call and took pictures and sent them to me. For real Rhonda! Yes babe I have reason to lie to you. Donna acted like she was tipsy on her way to the bathroom she stopped and said hello he didn't respond at all. So she texted me and told me what was going on. Okay Rhonda I hope you or your mother at least called the police to tell them of the threat. We did they came and took a report. They also told me to apply for a protective order. But the whole time while they were here I was thinking of you Victor. Really baby! Yes Victor.

I hope that Gabi fairs well. Should you need help in anyway please ask, I will help if I can. Thanks for the offer. Just please keep me in your prayers. I will. Please do me a favor don't hit me up for awhile. Why babe this is when we need each other more than anything. I no Vic! I just need some time.

Okay you hit me up when shit is better. Remember you're still my girl regardless and thanks again. Victor I know I told you not to contact me for a while but I thought for sure you would've for Valentine's if not then at least my birthday? I picked up my phone like 5 or 6 times to do that but I wanted to respect your wishes. See Victor that's why I'm so freaking crazy about you. You know I did write something for you. Let me hear them then. Hey beautiful I don't know if you've been following my posts this weekend but we did it.

Sold out the first batch of albums. Girl I'm on freaking cloud damn nine babe. I do have to admit I cried. Well Vic I have to say I want to see you, I've been so down and I knew the reason why I was. I realize that you're really my savior from all of this shit I've been dealing with. I wouldn't say savior because I'm not God but I will be there to help you change. So what are you doing Rhonda?

Im lying across my bed just took my shower. Waiting for you to get home so I can come over. I'm craving meatloaf babe. Well babe if you had said it early I would've made you some. What do you mean earlier? Exactly what I said I would've made you some and brought it over when I came over. But you didn't so you have to wait a day or two but I'll make you some. You'll do that for me babe? Yes when I told you I'd do anything for you I meant it. I know Victor but I've been hurt so many times in the past that I just see someone wanting to do all theses things for me and not wanting anything in return.

Rhonda we've always been like this towards one another from high school all the way to now. I've only lied to you twice and it hurt me more than you when you found out I did. I remember that day vividly Victor I told you I didn't want to have anything to do with you because your better than what I got home.

But you kept reassuring me the only reason why you did it was to protect me because you didn't want me in a corner crying. Yes I did say that but the look on your face and the sound of your voice I felt like a piece of shit. The walls I broke down and the trust I was gaining went down the drain. But in the long run you knew I wasn't doing it to hurt you and you forgave me. We actually became stronger behind that Rhonda.

Vic I never gave up on you I just need time and space quite a few times. I had to make sure this was the right thing. Even when I would lie to you never turned your back on me. I know I just wished you had told me the whole truth about the abuse because it wouldn't have lasted as long as it did babe. Well Vic I always told you I stayed because I had little kids mine were much younger than yours. So that stills not an excuse to neither allow someone to fucking kick your ass nor mentally abuse you either.

Yes Victor I know but I was thinking of the kids not my well-being. Damn girl we're gonna have to work on that because your never ever gonna have that feeling again. I hope so because talk is cheap and shit stinks if you don't wipe your ass. You got that right. Tell Gabi I said hello and I have her in my prayers. Will do and you do the same with your mom? Do you want me to come over to go with you to finish feeling out the paperwork for his restraining order?

Yes Vic I'll be by your house about 9:30-10 to pick you up. You haven't ridden in the Escalade since you dropped it off to me after you bought. Awe shit my girl is picking me up in the green beast. Yes I am. One last thing do you think that the reason why he's been fucking you up so much. Maybe but I'm not worried about him anymore because if he puts his hands on me again he'll be taken away in handcuffs. Yes that's right.

Well lil Jimmy is calling me so I'm gonna go now baby. See ya in the morning! Night beautiful! Stop it! Why Rhonda? Well if you keep that talk up I'm gonna have to suck your manhood out of you or is that what your trying to do Vic? Hell no! You like that big one eye snake and the way it makes you feel. Ummmmm yes I do but I can't talk like that right now because Lil Jimmy is standing in front of me.

Okay but I know your panties are soaking wet. You're an asshole, I hate you Vic. See I told you. Good night baby. Night. Jimmy what's wrong? Mommy can we talk and you have to promise me that you won't get mad at me for what I'm getting ready to say to you? I would never do that to you baby. What is it that you want to ask me? Are you sure you won't get mad at me? Yes Jimmy I always told you guys that you could come to me with anything. Mommy I heard the things my father was saying about you and it got me upset that he would say those hurtful things about you.

Well Jimmy sometimes people say things when they get upset but don't mean what their saying. Bullshit mommy! Excuse me little man do I need to spank your bottom? No ma'am! I just no that's a line of crap, here's what I wanted to ask you? What is baby? Well I know that your gonna get a divorce from my father before he kills you or us. Well I'm not sure about that right now. Here we go with that crap again mommy. Now James Simpson Jr, you have one more time to be disrespectful to me and I'm gonna wear your little ass out do you hear me? Yes ma'am! Mommy I know that Victor is Robyn's daddy and I want him to be mine as well.

Excuse me! Yes I said I really like him a lot and I see that he makes you very happy. Robyn always talks to us when she comes from over her dad's house about how much fun she had. She said that her father and stepmother might not be in love anymore but they still care for one another. Yes they do, so why did you decide to do this? I need someone in my life that's about something who loves my mommy and us as well. Well how do you think your father is gonna feel about all this.

Mommy in my eyes he's a man that slept with you to make kids. Jimmy that's not nice to say! Mommy that's how he makes us feel when your not here! He calls Robyn the lil nigger whore baby when your not here and cause us his ejaculation mistakes. No sir Jimmy! Mommy ask Auntie Donna she came by one day to pick Bree and I up she heard him going on about how he wish he didn't have you little ejaculation mistakes. Wow I'm sorry baby so so sorry!

Mommy if you want to leave him we all understand. I don't want to go over his parent's house either. They're so mean to us, but treat our other cousins like gold. His mother causes Robyn the nigger mutt, and nappy head tree monkey. Jimmy stop it right now? I can't take all this news it's hurting me so freaking much. Mommy if it's hurting you how do you think we feel, we're 16, 13, and 9 how do you think we feel. He's supposed to protect us and not say those things about you mommy nor us.

I don't know what to say, I can't believe what I'm hearing right now? I'm shocked, pissed, and broken hearted; everything has fallen apart in my perfect world. No mommy your world is just now starting we all know how crazy you are over Victor and we've grown to like him just as much as you. Robyn loves her biological father if only you knew mommy? Vic is at every one of mine and Bree's games no excuses about some NASCAR bull crap or wrestling.

Mommy I like wrestling but I'm only 9 years old he's 42 years old and he's liking it like he wish some man would throw him around like that. I know I pay attention to that myself, between nana myself and Victor we'll support all of your adventures as long as it's legal. Mommy I once heard Victor I mean daddies mom say it's better to walk with the king than being alone in torture. Yes his mother always had something nice or inspirational to say whenever you saw her.

She was such a wonderful person she used to sing this song I can't remember the name of the song. Jimmy you mean Just In Time. Yes mommy those words should mean so much to you right now because you're getting a second changes. Just like the song says, Just In Time, Jesus Step In, Just In Time. Do you think God put Victor back into your life now because he knew it wasn't a moment too late or too soon? Jimmy that's a good question! If I were a betting person I would have to say yes he did.

Well moms don't block whatever coming your way or ours. Mommy you need this as much as we do. Jimmy how did you get so smart? I've always been this way; remember I was the one who showed you how to use your Ipad when you got it. Yes your mommies bright little angel. Love you mommy stay strong. Oh my goodness that's what Victor says to me all the time. I know mommy.

Holy shit guys I'm tired but I can't put theses journals down especially Grams but I know G Pa's gotta have some good stuff in it as well. Yes it does if you don't believe me check out this journal entry from 1992 or 1993 while G Pa was attending Bethune-Cookman College. Okay we're all ears. Just one-question guy wasn't he kinda of annoying at times about Bethune-Cookman? Yes he was, it just ran through his veins. I often thought he loved that school more than us. Nope that's where your wrong Rhonda White Martin was what he loved more than anything.

If you don't believe here's a passage from his journal that I happened to come across when we we're here for Thanksgiving. March 6th 2012, I saw Rhonda today I almost forgot what today was but before she could say you forgot what today is, I shocked the shit out of her by saying happy birthday Rhonda. It had been a few years since we've seen each other in person.

Man she looks great after all theses years. I think I messed up when we didn't fight for one another. She seemed happy when I asked her about her life at home; I guess I did the same when she asked me. I knew mine was phony because Gabi wasn't doing well at all and the music business wasn't treating me kindly. But for some reason or another this day made a difference in both of our lives because soon after that day we were unbreakable.

I also found out for real the Robyn was my daughter and we bonded like I never left her life. I found myself wanting to talk to her more and more but most of all I saw that we wanted to be together again as one. I making her feel loved again and she's making me feel like she did 19 years ago before our lives changed. I think we both needed to marry others and have children with them as well to see that we needed one another. Well besides our daughter Robyn whom we both loved dearly.

It's scary that my feelings for her is crazy I'm still married but I want her I dream about her when I'm laying next to my wife, hell even when I'm doing the sheets dance with my wife I'm thinking its Rhonda. Gabi was thinking it was her that made me go down on her the way I did. But it wasn't! Don't get me wrong I loved Gabi but I had long lost the love. Rhonda and I would get together from time to time. This was going back to the time we spent making our daughter. But it wasn't the same because we had to sneak around then go back to our unhappy homes like nothing happened.

But it had been awhile since we both slept together. That night when I was on my way to the studio to lay down some track for my boy Lamone Andrews. She called me and asked me what I was doing? I told her I was on my to the Mix Factory in Stamford. I then asked her why, what's up? She said it's my birthday he forgot it once again. Then she started to cry a little, this would always get me. I think she kinda of knew this because she would do this knowing I would cave in. I told her I would see if I could do the tracks without Lamone or Bob being there, if so I would get a room at our special meeting place.

For those that don't know what that is, The Courtyard By Marriott. She agreed to meet there if I could goto the studio some other time. Now I'm torn between making some decent money for about 3 hours of work or speed time with the one woman that understood me. When I told the guys what was going on they told me to go see about her. I texted her to let her know I was on my way to see her. She reassured me that she would be at the hotel by the time I got there.

Bet your ass she was there in the room waiting for me. I'll never forget what she had on. Blue lose fitting yoga pants, a cream mesh top. As soon as I walked in she gave me a big hug, I knew she didn't have on any underwear because I saw her big tanned butt. She knew I saw it because she whispered in my ear babe I did all this for you. Now make this a memorable one for me please. Mind you every time we got together it was memorable.

But this time stood out the most from the room number 305 all the way to the date 2/5 maybe it was the blizzard outside. Whatever it was we talked about that particular night changed our lives forever. Not soon after this night I would be sitting in a hospital room watching her hanging on to dear life because of the physical abuse she had endured that evening at the hands of her then husband.

I hadn't cried that hard or hurt as much as I did since I found out that my wife Gabi was dying from cancer. I was torn between lovers that openly knew my feelings. Gabi had a sit down with the both of us and pretty much told her not to hurt me and for me to take care of Rhonda release her from that evil husband. When I say I had some awesome women and wives I truly mean it. Awwww! Gpa was such a sweetheart?
Dayvon he was but I wouldn't let any man that cared about me like that get away from me. Do you think their men like that out there for us? Yes cuz! Our mothers found men like GPa even my mom. Yes but she also screwed that up. V3 I think they both did but Dayna is just like her daddy so if she wants to fix it she'll do it, if not then I'm prepared to help my mom transition from

being a US Marshal to a civilian but most of all life as a single woman. Auntie Dayna will make it Dayvon. I hope so.

Back to gram's journal now. This one is from 2012-2013. I don't think I'll be able to handle this one guys. Why V3? This is all the bad, the ugly, and hurt in both life's. Cuz its gonna be okay. August 5th 2012 the man that should've been my husband birthday I want to reach out to him but I don't want to hear that bitches mouth. Forgive me God for saying that I know she's dying of cancer but I just wish she would let him go so I can have him. I can't stand being in this house anymore.

I'm afraid for myself as well the family. I swear God if he puts his hands on me again I'll kill him or I'll let Vic do it for me. I know that's not right to say but God send my baby my way cause I'm truly scared that he's gonna try and kill me. Rhonda who are you talking to it better not be that fucking jungle bunny? No Jimmy I'm just talking to God out loud. I think he's not listening to you anymore because he knows your into that baboons religion.

What's it called? Swing nigger swing. Your such a fucking asshole Jimmy. Why would you even say something like that to me? To be honest I'm emotionally drained from all of the years of mental and physical abuse that you bestowed upon me. Well the only way I'm letting you go is if God takes you away or I kill you bitch. Wow that's totally uncalled for. Bitch you're my property you better be glad this wasn't 100 years ago because your ass would've be stoned to death and that nigger well lets just say he would've been strange fruit.

I'm done I gotta go for a ride and get away from you. Where you goin? Gonna go and hang with that motherfucking spook? No I'm gonna goto my fathers grave and talk to him. You better be bitch because if I find your anywhere near that black nigger monkey I'm gonna beat you to you cant walk right or sit right do you hear me? Whateva James your so big and bad when it comes to me but when your comforted by a real man you act like a bitch? Well Rhonda try me and you'll see how much of a bitch I am?

Boy you'll learn someday you'll learn, I might have taken this shit before but I'm stronger, I'm wiser and thank God I made it. I know he's gonna remove me away from all this pain I'm receiving right now. I don't know when and don't know how but your not gonna be around much longer James Simpson. Mommy! Yes Rhonda! I'm going out for a little while I'll be back tonight though. You be safe out there, were are you going anyway?

Im going to daddies grave then taking a ride down to the shoreline to relax and do some thinking. Baby please be safe because my soul is telling me something bad is about to happen. I will mom I will! Let get my ass in my truck, I wonder if Vic is around? Hello! Are you busy babe? Nah what's wrong? Nothing I just needed to hear a loving voice. Okay something is bothering you Rhonda because I can tell in your voice. Victor can you meet somewhere? Babe I'll meet you wherever you want me too.

Okay I'm going to my dad's grave now can you meet me at the commuter lot in Cheshire? Yes I'll be there in about 45 minutes or so. Okay I'll see you then babe. Bye! Love you Rhonda! Good I get to see my baby, fuck what that prick said. God please watch out for me and my children. Like my mother I have a funny feeling in my soul that James is gonna try and harm us in some kind of way. I wonder if Donna feels like chatting a little? Hello Marcus is your mother home? Yes she is would you like to speak to her?

Yes baby but first how are you doin? I'm doing great I got accepted into Hampton and also FAMU. Oh that's great! But auntie I've decided to follow your husbands choice. What are you talking about that asshole didn't goto college he barely graduated high school. Not him, I'm talking about Victor. Silly that's not my husband, well not yet. I know that but I hear how you and mommy talking about him, he makes you happy.

Yes he does I wish I would've waited for him. Well your getting your chance right now. Boy your smart but that's up to him and God to see what happens. Well here's my mom auntie. Okay take care Marcus! I will! Hey Donna girl how you doin? I didn't catch you at a bad time did I? No girl I always have time for you, you're my homey from way back. I know this Donna but I know my whining can be a downer. No I know your going through a rough patch in your life. Girl I just gave it to God and I'm gonna walk with the king because he's got me covered.

Girl he sure does, sounds like you've been reading your bible or talking to Vic one? I've been doing both. He's such a breath of fresh air to my life, only thing that scares me is he's playing with my emotions, if he just wants to be fuck buddy we can but I hope not. Now see that's where your wrong you hold the keys to that Rhonda. You control that element if you want the dick, he's gonna give the dick and if you don't want it then he's gonna still be there for you.

Damn girl the brotha waited 20 years for you and your pussy so if he had to wait a little bit longer the pussy is always gonna be his. Wow you mean James ain't getting that pussy no more. Fuck no that little dick Irish boy can't do shit for me. So Rhonda here's what you need to do to see if Vic is just using you for pussy. The next time you see him look into his eyes and ask him the following questions, Victor R Martin Sr., since we've reconnected what are your feelings towards me please be truthful, next one Victor I need to be frank with you are you just using me for pussy or is the love you proclaim for me true?

Remember look him in the eyes when he answers theses questions. They are keys to his heart and soul. If he answers you without looking away or stumbling over his words then girl you betta go and get your man. Also stop that second-guessing and Pisces over analyzing shit. Thanks Donna for the advice because I'm meeting Victor in a little while after I go and visit my dad's grave. Oh boy what did that muthafucka do this time? Because the only time you go and visit your dad's grave by yourself is when he's off the chain.

Promises me you wont say anything to Victor before I see him. I won't Rhonda you know I don't get down like that anyway. True! Well he went totally off the deep end. He threaten me and the kids but this time he out right said he would kill me if he knew I was with that black porch monkey again. Oh my! What are you gonna do because that's serious. I know it is, but I'm scared if I get a protective order against him that he'll follow through with this threat.

Think about your mom and the kids. You'll need to be safe and if he's talking like that you need to get the hell up on out of there. Will you go with me to fill out the restraining order? Yes I will but I think you need to do that ASAP, because if he decides to do anything your covered and the police will be able to find him and charge him. I know it just hurt's my heart this man I've been with for the past 20 years or so wants to kill me because of my relationship with a old friend. Rhonda it's more than that, you've never stop loving him and remember he's the father of Robyn.

Yes but do you want your kids to grow up without you? No I don't! You got me crying over here now. Bree Bell, remember we've been friends since 2nd grade when my family moved her from Maryland. Yes we have that's why I trust you with this stuff. I'm just scared of what Victor will do to him if he does something to me? Well I wouldn't be that concerned with that because Victor isn't gonna get his hands dirty with his shit but he'll damn sure will get some of his thug friends to do him. Let's not forget he's got deep connections in a few police departments in our area.

I know, I know, do you think it will get that far Donna? Shit ya if you don't get that protective order. Hey I gotta go that's Victor calling me on the other line. Okay go handle your business and give me a call later on. I will donna. Hey baby you okay? Yes! I was on the phone with Donna talking about us and him. So what's so important that you needed to meet me now. I don't want to discuss it right now but when I see you in a few minutes

I'll share with you everything I promise you Victor I'll tell you everything babe. You sure! The last time you were suppose to tell me and you thought sucking my dick would get my mind off of it?

Well did it Victor? Yes baby it did, I just don't understand why you left right away when you were done? Vic I wanted the smell of your cock still in my mouth when I went home to kiss James on the mouth. No you didn't do that Rhonda? Yes da fuck I did, an I enjoyed every minute of it. That's why he says all that crazy shit like he does to you babe.

Nah Victor, he's not worthy of me nor of the love I've given him over the last twenty plus years. Now Rhonda when I said that about Gabi you went the fuck off on me especially in her present condition. I sure did but your relationship is totally different. You didn't come looking for me I came looking for you. At first all I wanted was someone to laugh and hang with but the more I was around you I knew I had to have you all the way. Everyday I look at our daughter and say to myself why am I here? She's so happy when she's over your house even how Gabi accepted her as her own.

Victor what woman wouldn't want to be with a man that makes her feel the way I feel when I'm with you. True indeed babe. But I'm not trying to break up your home either Rhonda. Victor my home was broke long before you really came back into my life. I don't understand but I guess you're the only one that knows what you want. Hey babe I gotta go that's Dayna on the other line I'm at the commuter lot already so I'll see you when you get here.

Okay Vic I love you baby. Love you too Bree Bell. Well Ms. Rhonda it seems like you have a few things that you need to clear up. If I stay with James he'll probably end up killing me, but if I decide to be with Victor is he gonna change like James did? That's something that only God and I will have to figure out. Who are you talking Rhonda? Nobody gram! Just talking out loud. How are you doing? I'm doing okay gram just have a lot going on in my life right now. I heard your mom told me some of it but I wanted to hear it from you first hand. Gram you don't need to hear my sob story. Rhonda you're my grandbaby an I know when all of my grandchildren aren't themselves.

An baby you haven't been yourself for awhile. That's not true gram. Yes it is! Rhonda non stare qui giaceva a tua nonna perche saro battuto il culo proprio come ho fatto quando eri piccolo. Gram why are you yelling to me in Italian? You wouldn't understand my happiness I have right now anyway. Oh girl I know about that jigga boo you've been running around with as well. Gram that's not nice at all. I didn't want my daughter marrying no damn sambo and I'll be damn if you have a porch monkey swinging from our family tree. I'm so glad your grandfather isn't alive to hear of your whorish ways with that cazzo moulinyan nero!

Gram please stop that talk. I came to you for guidance but it seems like your just as worse as James. Baby you need for your husband to battere la puttana fuori di voi. Oh my god gram I cant believe you just said that to me. Yes I did Rhonda. I don't understand your generation you'll do anything to get one of those gold chain wearing monkey's an when they start beating your ass or messing up your credit then you want to come back home crying. Gram that's not true at all. Your wrong with that statement, if you want to be correct that's che white trash bastardo! Yes gram I speak it just as fluent as you. Has messed up my credit stole from me and even cheated on me. So why should I stay here, I'm not happy I cry all the time to the point I wish that God would just take me away from this hell hole.

Then I figured it out he was allowing to get out of the situation all together. Victor is my savior. I'm gonna let God show me if this is true or not gram. Well baby if you let that fried chicken watermelon eating coon into my family I'll never speak to you again. Gram then I guess this is gonna be one of the last times I speak to you then. It's breaking my heart that my family would be happy that I found myself again. But no only mommy and the kids are. I have to go gram I hope you think long and hard about what you said. I love you regardless of what you think of Victor and I's relationship.

Baby I love you too, I hope to see you soon. Only if you change your views will I. I'm old an I'm stuck in them Rhonda. Bye baby! Bye gram. Now I'm really stuck God, I know what Victor and I are doing is going totally against your teachings but for some reason you brought him back into our life's. Robyn is so happy to be loved by her real dad, my other two love him like he's theirs as well. Mommy sees how happy he makes me feel. I haven't felt this way in years.

Hell he even got going me back to church. I really love it when he takes me with him and Gabi to their church. It's something about the way the spirit moves through me when I'm hearing Boo Boo Barnes preach. He's so eloquent with the way he speaks of God's word. Boy can he sing. I love when he has Victor get up and sing Just In Time with him. Lord I'm giving it to you to lead me down the right path. Where the hell did I park that damn car at, it should be easy for me to find by now. Oh there it is my baby bought my green Jaguar.

I wonder what he's driving today it's nice out also Sunday as well. I guess I'll have to wait and see. Hey babe I'm almost there where are you parked at? Hey sexy, I'm parked right at the entrance in the blue ghost. I was hoping you were driving that.

Can we go to West Haven Beach when I get there? Yes babe we can. Something must be really messing with you because you only want to go there when you really need my attention Rhonda? Victor I got so much shit going on in my head that I just need to vent.

So if I start to yell or cry just hold me in those strong arms of yours. What did I tell you from day one of us getting back together Rhonda? Yes you did but I don't just assume that you will do that for me. Rhonda that's were your wrong I'll do what I gotta do to make you happy. Even if that means for us to break this off I'll do that. Victor don't say that babe, I'm at the light right now I'll be there in a second. I see you. Your wearing my favorite color.

Of course I am Victor. Why did you do that Rhonda? I thought maybe if I did that you might want me even more. Rhonda I don't need the color purple to dictate how I want you. Like our song back in high school. Nah Vic not Lately. Yes Rhonda, Look into my eyes, What I'm going through, might see something you like a paradise for two me and you. Yes Victor. I want you bad Victor but I'm so damn confused. When you say you want me is in the physical or wholeheartedly? Damn it Vic I want both. But after today's visit with my grandmother really has me twisted.

Why is that babe? Well she basically said if I ended my marriage with James and did anything with you that she disown me. Baby you knew that this wasn't gonna be pretty. Your family still thinks that James is the father of Robyn. How are gonna explain to them that he wasn't her father and that we've been messing around off and on for the past 20 years? Well that's for me to figure out at the right time. I guess so Rhonda. You look very damper today Vic.

How is Gabi doing today? You know I'm pissed off at you for getting Robyn that damn Lincoln. You could've got he a Kia or Hyundi. No damn 18 year old college freshman needs to be driving a fifty thousand dollar car. Okay then I'll take hers back and your Jaguar as well. Da fuck you will Victor that's my baby that you bought me. Hell I don't even fart in there. I see! I got a question for you Rhonda? Shoot! What are we really doing? I've contemplated our relationship for a minute now. Basically every since we all went out to dinner. Vic, I've been thinking the same.

But after today's fight with him and gram saying those hurtful words about our present relationship has made it quite clear that I'm ready for us babe. I don't give a flying fuck who disagrees with our love. Neither do I Rhonda, I felt that way more than 19 years ago when you got pregnant with our daughter Robyn. Well what's your next move then? I know, I know, I have to file for my divorce.

Yes Rhonda but you need to get that damn restraining order in play first because if you don't that man you left me for 22 years ago is gonna hurt you. If he does that Rhonda trust and believe I wont be nice at all. I know your temper Victor and I must say I feel honored that you would sacrifice your freedom to get rid of him but I would totally lost without you. That's why I would never put myself in that type of predicament babe. Tell me more about your visit with your nana? Well it was going fine until the last 30-45 minutes. We got on the subject of James and I's marital problems.

She acknowledged that she knew what was going on in my household from the fighting to how I'm not sleeping with James anymore. Wait how did she find all this out? My mom talks to her about everything. But her views are totally different of her own mother. Yes your mother loves me and the way I treat you. Yes Victor we sit up a lot of nights talking about you over a few glasses of wine.

Well damn I feel honored. Silly why? Because after all theses years and the two of us having our own life's that you would still sit and talk to your mom about me. Victor I never shared this with you before. But mommy loves the fact that you remember her birthday as well as mother's day. That bastard has long stop doing any of that for her. I barely get anything from him. But on his days he expects for me to suck his penis and give him some. Why you say his penis. Trust you have a dick, cock, love stick, he has a penis.

To be honest Vic once you and I started back sexing on a regular when I was giving him some ass I couldn't feel him. Now that big ole yella cock you got my vajayjay gets all moist just thinking of it. Okay I guess that's cool with me babe. So what else did your nana have to say? That she truly didn't like the fact I was with you because of your race. Well I'm sorry I was born with this skin. Your a freaking asshole at times Vic.

Why would you say that about me? Because I'm trying to be serious then you say shit like this. Rhonda calm down I was just making a statement. I know you don't look at color nor race babe. Yes I don't, I look at character, and trust, and behavior. Well I'm not trying to be an asshole babe why did you choose him over me then? His behavior was so predictable from the mental to physical abuse. Victor I never said I was perfect. Look at your relationship Vic, with Gabi the emotional things she did to you.

Yes that's true I could fix her emotional abuse towards me. But you have to remember I found out why Gabi was doing that? She was battling cancer. Yes Victor but I heard all of the whining from you. True! Rhonda it still doesn't weigh like what you've gone through. Victor I love the fact you've been there for me but I don't blame you if walk away from me because I can be so wishy-washy. It's not that love you've gotten so use to being treated that way.

Oh baby hush can you turn that up. Why I don't hear what's on nor am I paying attention to it. Shit that's that new joint from Lamone, To Please You. Yep it sure is the boys out did themselves with this song. Speaking of music Vic, when is the album coming out and don't bullshit me? Why would you say something like that to me? I know when you fucking lying to me. Babe what did I say or do for you to change like that? Nothing, don't mind me I'm just being that typical Pisces's. that's getting kinda of old now Rhonda that's like the little boy that always cried wolf and when it came time for someone to believe him they didn't.

Not  saying I wont but it'll be hard for me to do so if you keep talking to me that way. I lied to you that one time over 5 years ago and you haven't let me forget about it to this day. Why is that? Babe you know all the shit I've been through and with the bullshit my own nana said to me today is fucking killing me on the inside. The only people that believe in me is my secret love affair with a black male an my mommy.

Rhonda just get what you need done and fuck what everyone else thinks or says about us. See that's easy for you to say Vic because of your personality, you demand respect in order for you to give it back. I cant do that when I do folks think I'm a bitch or worse a cunt. Wow, wow, wow, there's no need for that language Rhonda. I'm just expressing myself babe don't be such a bitch Victor. Better yet Victor come here and give me a kiss, I wanna feel your strong muscular body against mine. I haven't seen Vic for 3 weeks but a lot happen during this time.

My nana's health went down hill big time. The last conversation I had with her I told her I didn't want to see anymore if she didn't accept Victor and I's relationship. She asked to see all of her grand and great grandchildren the day before she expired. When she got to me she asked everyone to leave the room. I thought it was gonna be another yelling match. It wasn't she apologized and said she was wrong judging Victor the way she did and that if he makes you happy then you have my blessings. We laughed, we cried, but most of all we made our peace.

She did warn me on getting away from James because it would end ugly if I didn't. This was August 31$^{st}$ she passed labor day September 1$^{st}$. I couldn't believe she wasn't here anymore now I just have two Vic and mommy. God don't take them from me. The first person that I saw and I love this was Gabi at the grocery store after my nana passed. She saw me and said bitch why are you looking such a wreck? I knew she was joking but I busted out crying. She thought I was crying for what she called me. But it wasn't. I told I had just lost my nana.

She came over and gave me a hug and said if I needed anything to let her know. She also told me that her cancer was under control, but I knew wasn't true because Vic had told me that they weren't giving her that much longer to live. Was it divine intuition or what but Victor called right as I was walking away. I told him my nana had passed. He was sorry to hear that she did. But was upset that we didn't make peace with our argument.

I told  him that we did as well as her giving me her blessing on our relationship. He told me if I needed anything to give him a call. I told him thanks and that he should give my mom a call. Now when I tell you that the next few weeks were hell I mean they were hell. Dayvon is this leading up to her near death incident with James? Yes Raven! I don't want to hear this part so I'm gonna excuse myself while you guys read this. Why cuz? Because I don't want to hear how our grandmother almost died at the hands of that crazy ass man. Hey this is suppose to be a healing period part in her life so we're gonna have to read about that night.

November 15th started off like any other Saturday running kids to games talking to my babe Victor on phone going grocery shopping with mom. As usual mister man at home not doing a fucking thing at home. I had made plans to hang out with Donna before coming home to cook dinner. But on my way home with my mom I received a call from Victor he was somewhat upset.

I asked him what was the problem? He said that he need to see. I told him I didn't have any free time today could it wait until tomorrow after he got out of church. I could tell in the tone of his voice that he didn't like that answer. Rhonda I can't wait you need to make yourself available to me today. I had a weird dream last night I'm scared something bad is getting ready to happen to one of us. Stop being so freaking silly Victor.

Nothing is gonna happen to us. Like I said we can see each other tomorrow after you get out church. No Rhonda, no I can't wait that long girl. Okay Victor I'll see what I can do. Well let me know soon I'm getting ready to go into the studio I should be done in about an hour or two. I will give you a call when I get out Rhonda. Okay Vic! I love you babe. Boy was that a dumb mistake, the next time I would see that man would be November 17th when he was laying at the foot of the bed asleep.

 I looked over at my mother to see if this was true. She told me he didn't leave my side the whole time you were sleeping. What happened why am I in here? Rhonda you don't remember anything? No mommy, What happen? James finally snapped Saturday after we got back from shopping. I remember him arguing with me in the driveway then the next thing I remember hearing somebody saying we're loosing her. Hello my sweetheart!

I thought I was gonna lose you babe. I'm still not understanding everything mom. Rhonda, James finally snapped. I told you I had a bad feeling Rhonda and you told me not to worry about it. Victor all that matters is you're here right now when I need you. Yes Rhonda, keep on walking with the king and things truly will turn around in our favor. I hope Victor, I really hope so. I'm gonna step out so the kids can come in and see you.

Wow the kids our here Vic? Yes they are, your mom brought them with her. I rode with you in the ambulance. You did Victor that was sweet of you. I wasn't gonna let you pass and I not be there. Please be strong for our daughter, she's been crying every since you left in the ambulance. Victor I have to say this about you, you've been such a great person since coming back into my life. I guess now I'm free of all the strive? Yes you are Rhonda. Here comes the kids I'm gonna step out for a few I'll be back in when their done visiting you. I can't take this cuz.

Why Raven? Like I told you before Dayvon I didn't want to hear this. It's because of my mother why gram was almost killed. Auntie Robyn might have seen a lot of that hate but this man was evil way before G Pa and gram laid down to create her. Hey mommy since you were there that day, can you tell us how it felt seeing your mother hanging on to dear life at the hands of your step-father? Wow I never thought I would be sharing any of this with my nieces and nephews let alone my daughter.

If it wasn't for my biological father and nana, I would've lost it. Victor and Rhonda's bond was very strong at that point they were practically living together. The asshole just was there in body but not in person. He treated me like a nigger, porch monkey, nigger lovers baby. Mommy caught hell, beatings, psychological abuse. I saw a strong mother that was loving to me by the time lil Jimmy was born she was a bitter depressed lady that was scared all the time. But then she would go out from time to time after theses outings she would come home smiling, singing, like her old self.

I didn't know at the time nor did my siblings know why? Victor was there and had been there since September 1994. Who would of thought getting a social security number would bring them back. Yes mom that's true, but there were times that I wished they never had me. It was great when he thought I was white then came puberty for me when I went from looking like a cute little Italian princess to a pretty light skinned black girl.

He notice the complexion change and the hair. Asked mommy if he was the father by now the peace was long gone from that household. She told him yes and that we've been sleeping together for the last 13 years. Every time I found out I was pregnant after Robyn I wondered who the father was. I can honestly say the other two are yours but they love him more than you. Your own son is scared of you. You've taught them its okay to beat, mentally and physically abuse whomever they're dating.

I myself struggled with a relationship like that while I was in college then my big bother and sister helped that situation out or shall I say they whipped that muthafucka's ass big time. Mommy did he ever try to hit great nana? He treated her like shit but he had good sense. That ole school Greek woman would've cut his balls off then feed them to her. Yes nana was a strong woman, and wanted the best for us girls.

Mommy was it hard for you to adjust being a mixed child once you found out. It was as long as that man was around. He really hated me as much as he did my beloved mother Rhonda. If it weren't for my mothers, step sister Dayna and daddy. I would've gone through with my suicide attempt but they taught me to love myself. Dayna and I being of the same heritage helped me, she said be proud of both.

I did all through out my teens and early twenties I looked for a man like my dad but it seemed like I was more drawn towards men like James Simpson. Until my sophomore year at Bethune-Cookman I was dating this sigma my first mistake. You crazy auntie, what did the great Victor R Martin have to say about that? You know your grandfather, he went ape shit on me. Well it was around Black College Reunion or Freaknik, I wanted to go out with my roommates this guy told me he forbid me to go out. I told this black bastard that only my mother and father could speak to me in that tone. He slapped the shit out of me, we fought for the next half and hour or so. Now mind you your grandfather was alum but your Aunt Dayna as well as your Uncle VJ. Word had gotten back to the Ques on campus because both of them being bruh's. They came over to have a talk with him. Auntie and mommy don't you mean an ass whipping.

Well yes! Auntie Dayna was a Delta so some of her soror's contacted her of what they had heard. Dayna called me and heard my tone and new something was defiantly wrong with me. I kept telling her everything was okay don't come I'm fine. Well if y'all haven't figured out by now that your family has this thing called the F it switch some folks call it the Sue Martin coming out. Yes mommy I heard that and have experienced myself. Before I knew it my brother and sister were there.

They sat down with Leroy Jackson and myself. VJ told him the next time he puts his hands on my baby sister I will blow your muthafucking brains out. Now your Auntie Dayna took a totally different avenue. My big sis said dude fuck with her again you'll never have to worry about touching another woman because once my cousin Prince Bond gets through fucking in the ass with his big ole horse dick and turn you out only thing your gonna be able to worry about shitting right.

What did G Pa and gram have to say about all of this? I don't remember everything but soon after that they decided to get me something off campus for me. But getting back to that night guys. Mommy had a hard time taking everything in, this man she loved and cared for at one time had totally flipped out. The man she should've married wanted to do for her but was still married just like she was. Cool thing about it he never left her side. Mom stayed in the hospital for about 10 days or so. She had broken ribs, lower back pain as well as a broken nose.

Pardon me mom but holy shit she was able to trust again after all that? Yes guys my mother was a strong woman once her and Victor became a fulltime item. She was in the hospital when James was arraigned the next day, but Dayna, Nana, VJ, and Gabi were there to see that scum being presented in court with that damn orange jumpsuit on. Really G Pa's first wife was there? Yes they became very close just before she passed away.

Gabi was a strong woman let her man goto his original love and friend her as well. From what I heard he looked far worse than mommy did. You see your grandfather had a lot of pull. They beat the living shit out of him. James ended up getting 10 years suspended after 8 years served. During those 8 years my biological parents broke up, lost twins and married. The hardest part on the six of us was when Mom and Dad lost Raven and Ravon.

Mommy had gone back into a depressive state pushing everyone away. She thought God was punishing her for her adultery, it was even rumored that she was gonna reconcile with James. Then came the demise of my Step-Mother Gabi.

Lil Jimmy and mommy were coming home from his baseball game they had stop to get some pizza from Nino's to celebrate his no hitter game as well as his last game. Jimmy asked her if he could go by and see daddy. I don't know if it was divine intervention or what but she said yes. Mommy said she was excited to see daddy as well. When she turned onto G Pa's street her excitement was overwhelming. But he wasn't there, she was upset thinking he was on a date or something.

But by the time she had gotten home I had called her to let her know that Gabi had passed away.

The scream and yell that came out of my Mother's mouth I'll never forget. She quickly gave the phone to nana who also let out the same scream. Lil Jimmy got on the phone I told him what happened I heard mommy in the background saying tell your dad I was on my way. Like I said it was divine intervention, that very night they got back together and stayed with one another until she found Victor R Martin Sr, in the studio doing what he loved best.

I'll never forget that phone call I heard that scream and yell it was 30 years ago all over again. This time it was my Daddy. Daddy was gone. My heart dropped to the bottom of my soul. Mommy and Daddy meant so much to me now she's all by herself no more Victor in the house. Everyone thought she was crazy walking around the house talking to him after he passed. But it was the bond the two of them had for one another. They healed one another, I remember I had to be about 14 or so I had met this boy from West Haven my daddy told me no boyfriends until I was 16 but I was a hot tale girl.

Everything they told me not to do I did. It was about November or so I was late I was scared as hell because not only was the biological were gonna find out but the steps as well. James finally found out before mom and dad did. I was home from school because I was feeling under the weather. I kept throwing up, James was like you're a whore just like your mother. Wow no he didn't mom? Yes he did! So why did you tell them or did they figure it out? Well guys mom showed a little sympathy but Victor Sr, went in on me.

He didn't speak to me for weeks because he was so heart broken. Awww! Mom what got him to forgive you? My daddy held grudges but when it came to the kids he would always come around. It just took him a little longer this time. But mommy wasn't she held my hand explained to me she was upset with me but we're gonna work through all this. She told me I was to young to have the child I had a lot of life left in front of me. We agreed for me to terminate it. So mommy what happened to the boy? Well that's another story, your grandfather took care of that problem.

No mommy he didn't! Yes he did guys Victor's greatest pleasure was breaking down the enemy in any means necessary. My father had a really ugly side; scary at times. But that was my only thing that hurt them when I younger. But mommy started really seeing a change in James the abuse was out of control. Then that day, I've seen my dad cry only 4 times the lost of his grandmother the day Dayna and I getting married lastly his on marriage to mommy.

But he was so hurt seeing his beloved Rhonda lying there almost lifeless. Step mother dying of cancer and mommy almost lifeless because of James's hate. Mom enough I told you guys I didn't want to hear about this. Raven come outside with me for a minute. Why Mommy? Look I said bring your ass on that's why baby? What if I don't want to Mommy? Girl you maybe 21 years old but I'll still beat your ass. Did you forget who my mother was? No ma'am I didn't forget. Well then I would find it in your best interest that you come outside then. Yes ma'am! Raven I understand that you don't want to hear about what my mother endured it needs to be told damnit.

Mommy I understand but I don't want to hear all about it because she almost died at that man hands. My question if this all and great FUCKING Victor R Martin Sr, cared so much why didn't he do something about after you found out that he was your real dad? Raven I asked the same thing every time that man verbally abused her. I told my daddy as well as my stepmother Gabi. They just told me if I felt like if he was gonna harm my mommy to call the police. I did do that a couple of times but they didn't do anything. Come take a report or tell him to leave, but never arrested him because he never laid hands on her.

The kicker was when he pulled his gun out on her, put it up right to her head and said I blow your nigger loving brains all over this muthafucking floor you nigger loving whore. Yes Raven, before you even ask I called 911. The operator heard him making the threats but that didn't even get him arrested. But when my parents moved south into this beautiful house that we're standing in front of right now. You guys were little maybe 2 or three when they moved in.

Your Grandfather and Grandmother were in the driveway playing and tripped the motion sensors next thing they knew guns were drawn on them he was forced down to ground and arrested. This was they're property and he was treated like a common criminal. But that bastard stepfather of mine fucking threaten to kill my mom, nana, and myself because of her being a nigger lover, a nigger lovers Mother, and me being the nappy headed monkey created in that union.

Since you cleared that up for me mommy I'll go back inside to finish hearing about it. Hey guys I'm back! Is everything okay with you and Auntie Robyn? Yes mommy just had to bring me back down a notch or two. We know how those Martin genes can be. So where were we? G Pa at the hospital with Gram. It seems like they're love grew more after that this one particular incident than anything else.

Even the birth of my mommy and them getting married. Gram was such a brave woman as well as a coward to allow that man do what he did. Wow Dayvon that's really fucked up to say. Well it's the truth and sometimes the truth can kick you in your fucking throat. True, but I would've said it in a different way. What if your mother or Auntie Calven came downstairs and heard you say that? Oh the da fuck well. Like I said before sometimes the truth hurts. An one thing this family knows is hurt and truth.

Damn Dayvon your really going in right now. I think we need to take a break go find Uncle VJ's secret stash and have a cipher. I'm down for that and I know exactly where he keeps it at. Where would that be at Raven? The damn pool house just like G Pa used to. Hey sis! What was all that yelling going on outside earlier? Your niece trying me. I hope you didn't get all Sue Martin on her? No Dayna!

I just had to bring her down a notch or two. Mommy didn't like for us to carry on this way so I hope you were able to straighten out what ever the two of you were arguing about. Yes we did, but I refuse to have that child or any child think they can talk to me any ole kind of way. I don't give a good damn if your 25 or 65. If you're my child or niece or nephew your gonna give me respect. True Robyn, but if memory serves me right I remember you trying not only mommy and daddy but also mommy Gabi on several occasions.

Yes I did and I got the shit beat out of me as well. That may be true, but don't be so hard on them remember we're all grieving over mommy's loss. I know I still can't believe it. How's Calven doin? She hasn't said anything to anyone since we got here two weeks ago? Well as the oldest sibling I've tried several times to speak to her, but to no avail. Hell lil Jimmy is just as bad Dayna. I saw him in passing, asked him how he was doin and handling mommy's death he just said I'm fine went into his room and started crying.

You gotta realized they are the babies of the family and spent more time with the two of them then we did. Yes they did but we all miss her and the glass of wine. Yep then she would sit and talk shit all night or until she got sleepy. Mommy where are you? Im in the kitchen with Auntie Robyn. Why, what's up? We're getting ready to go out for a cipher you wanna come out and smoke? There's no trees here? Yes there is!

Where at and whose is it? C'mon now mom you know whose it is? Your Uncle VJ is gonna kill y'all. Damn it Dayna why you think they asked you to come out? I know why, but I need some herb to calm my nerves right about now. I'm coming too then! Hey where are y'all off to? Just outside to the pool house why VJ? I'll kill'em! No you won't VJ! They got it honestly from they're grandparents, and us. But why my stash? Shit VJ everyone knows you got that good shit. True! Then if your going out to smoke my shit then I'm coming out to smoke it as well.

Dayvon whose that coming outside? Nobody! That's why we don't smoke with you and your paranoid ass. Up yours I'm not paranoid not one bit. But I know that's your mom and Uncle VJ coming down here right now. Your shitting me! Nope, here they come right now. He's gonna kill us for going into his secret stash. Hey Uncle VJ! What's up? So y'all had the nerve come out here get into my secret stash without asking me. Nah it's like that!

Wait before you answer that with a stupid answer remember your already smoking the evidence. Okay it was me who convinced them to come out here Uncle VJ. It would be one of Dayna's kids. Why you say that? You can answer that one big sis! Your uncle used to do the same to me when I was away at school then lie and say mommy or daddy found it. Now Gabi smoked because of her cancer, but Vic was a cognac drinker so we all thought.

But that dude smoked trees or as he called it Reefer. You could always tell when he did to growing up. He was naturally funny but once he had that. I'm telling you he was off the chain. Do we have any hamburgers or steaks? Why mommy? Shit it's nice out why don't we make the best of the weather and cook-out? See there goes the spirit of

Victor R. Martin, Sr. he would find any find of way to have family over to cook-out as well socialize with the ones he loved the most.

I can remember growing up Uncle VJ, during the summer a majority of the grand kids would be here. After church every Sunday Gram and G Pa would let us go swimming while they cooked on the grill outside. Before long neighbors would be over as well as church members just having a grand ole time. Now that the 2 of them are gone its weird doing this without hearing that laugh or them trying to sneak off to do whatever they did. Well we all know what that was that little horn dog Gram of ours was always trying to bang his brains out.

Yes that was very true Dayvon! Only thing I can tell y'all is be thankful for the time you had with them. I had my mommy who loved me unconditionally as well as my biological father. But I really didn't see the real love they had for until that fateful day when I finally found out that Victor was my dad and that fucking bastard my mom was married too wasn't. From that day on it seemed like they tried their best to make it better for me. Right Dayna? Yes even though Gabi nor Rhonda weren't my biological Mothers they treated me like I was theirs.

That's why the death of both of them hurt me so much. I was taught how to be a woman as well as a real Mother to my children. I may have had some hick ups in my marriage but that was no fault of theirs nor my dad as I would always put the blame on. My lessons learned in life was this saying I used to hear daddy say around the house. It went like this some men and women walk around life with they're eyes closed but never knowing once the opened eye happens you'll truly find that our love will never die.

Damn I haven't heard that in years big sis. Dad always had something encouraging to say to you if you were willing to listen. Yes Robyn, I know you miss him a lot. Because I caught you talking to his picture last night. Yes Im guilty of that. Us girls were the highlight of his day, it wasn't a day that he didn't call all four of us. Yes! sometime trying to start some shit. Like I don't know why that damn Calven talking junk about you Dayna.

Yes! how bout when daddy was working on Uncle Bob's album and he had Bree tell him that he was stuck in Texas because they didn't let light skin folks fly on planes after 4pm in the afternoon. Yes he really could get you going. VJ why don't you put on some music? okay guys any request? Nope just play some music. Who here remembers the trip across country when they first got the tour bus? I do!
Yes Ravon you should because between you and my Raven I thought mom was gonna beat the black out of the two of you. That's not true Uncle VJ. Bullshit Ravon I remember my mom tightening up you guys ass a couple of times. So mom why didn't you stop her? Ya Robyn why didn't you.

Oh now all of you have forgotten that chick wasn't wrap tight. Yes she was but nana was on the trip with us she would've saved you. She would but I'm like this if y'all needed discipline who am I to say no mom don't do that. Her status on the ladder of life was higher than mine. Like now I'm higher than yours with my grand-kids. If you don't get in their asses I will bring the funk out and tear up some ass. Yes ma'am I know.

Oh shit turn that up aint nothing like cooking out and listen to Marvin Gaye's Got To Give It Up. Can you remember how this would get that fool dancing and talking shit. Yes! God forbid if Uncle Shawn or them were over, that was straight comedy. Better than comedy, I can remember one time they debated over the damn Alphabet and the right way of saying it.

We damn near died from laughter. Yes, we did little brotha! See you guys were lucky to have them at an older age. But the six of us knew the struggle and the hurt of death and abuse. Wow is that uncle Jimmy I hear? Yes! I heard all of y'all out here I was wondering what was going on so I came out to be nosey.

While walking over to the pool house I heard y'all reminiscing about our parents. I can remember when Calven was on her way home from Bethune-Cookman an was almost killed in a bad car crash. The state police came to the house to notify them of the accident. He called the black trooper a uncle tom and the white trooper a sambo.

Then told them if they didn't get out of his house he was gonna hurt one of them. I was in stitches, but understood his pain at the same time. So what happened after that Lil Jimmy? Mom and dad went to the hospital and didn't leave her side the whole time she was there. The fucked up thing about that whole situation I was suppose to be with her but I decided to fly home at the last minute.

I was in so much pain seeing her lying in that hospital with all those wires and monitors hooked up to her. Mommy didn't understand why I was acting the way I was at the time but Vic knew and pulled me to the side and told me theses encouraging words to this day I still stand by and share with my students. Now Jimmy this isn't your fault nor fault of God but his blessings and love that you have for sister will never die. You have to stay strong for her because she needs positive around her not this.

You may feel guilty but its not. Jimmy I want you to go in there be strong for her please give off positive vibes and let her know that your there for her. Granted I've changed some of the wording over the years. But I always kept the strong, the positive, every time I think of those talks I think of where we've all come from and How life truly changed for the better because of their union.

Yes lil bro your right. If weren't for those Closed Eyes or Opened Eyes after all of that abuse she endured I don't think we would be here sharing Our Love towards them with our own children and grand and in Dayna's great-grand. Watch it Jimmy! Dayna embrace the fact that you're a beautiful looking great-grand. You don't look old enough to have a grand-child let alone a great grand. I have say your right on that one Lil Jimmy. See that damn Victor R Martin Sr. can still work magic from the grave. This is all he ever wanted. Why do you say that Jimmy?

Remember Calven and I were the last ones at home and the youngest. They would sit around the pool at the old house back in Connecticut once all of y'all would leave and go back to wherever you were living at the time. An talk about once they have gone on home to be with God, would we still be as close or would we be divided?

To be honest with all of you I wouldn't be the mother I am now if it weren't for my mother and step-mother they made me into the woman I am today Calven Martin and if I could be just a portion of them I'll fill humbled. Hey big bruh how do you feel about all of this? What are your views on your parents? Do you want my honest opinion or the sugar coated version?

Dad told it like it is please remember we're writing this so that the world will know the truth about the Martin's and Simpson's union. Okay if you say so! I hated the both of them, my father because he was unfaithful to my dying mother and Rhonda because she just couldn't say no to his advances.

Then came Robyn, I love my sister but I think that was the icing on the cake. Not only did this already dysfunctional family crumble now we have the dirty little secret that was hidden for years. Damn! Daddy your not holding any punches on this one. No I'm not you guys said you wanted the truth how I felt and I'm gonna speak my mind.

This guy I looked up to him, from being a hard worker sometimes working 2 or 3 jobs at one time to provide for us as well as coaching basketball and belong to his social and fraternal organizations.

Yes he did do that VJ! But why are you so mad about the other things? Look you guys don't get a boy learns to be a man from his father. From how to dress to how your suppose to treat your wife or girl. Only thing I learned was it okay to chase ass and have outside children. VJ, we all understand your feelings remember we all saw it as well.

My mommy smiling when ever she saw or talked to your dad, but hated our own father with a passion. Fuck she cheated on him from before they even got married with Victor… ie… Robyn Martin. Yes my parents were unfaithful to they're own mates and had me.

I hated growing up in a house that no love was shown to me by a man that I thought was my biological father and then when I found out who my real one was I see the lavish lifestyle he was living compare to ours. Mommy worked her ass off only to have that low life step father of mine steal mommy's money and the abuse I don't even want to bring that up again. Yes that's cool Robyn.

But this man fucked me up for years. I thought I was suppose to cheat on my kids mother. I loved this woman with all my heart but I wanted more and more. We almost got divorced not once but three times because of my shit. I finally had to go and get help for my habits. I must say it was the best thing I ever did. I was able to not only save our marriage but show my own children the proper behavior of a married man. Granted Victor Martin Sr., did the same once they got married and I'm proud of him for that.

Now on the other hand when it came to teaching all of us about business that's where I have to say he is and was the best. Look at it he took a dream and made it into a multimedia empire in the African-American community. Yes they did do that. Funny thing all of my aunties and uncles haven't said was that damn love for Bethune-Cookman.

I can remember I was in my senior year of high school in New York. Mommy and I were talking about schools, she asked me what I wanted to study? I told I wasn't sure but I knew I wanted to goto a HBCU. She was very excited about that. We then went into which schools I was interested in going I said of course Cookman, but I also had interest in FAMU, Hampton, Morgan State, Delaware State, and Norfolk.

She said to me its your choose but don't mention FAMU you around your grandfather. I agreed with her.
So I say it had to be about four or five weeks later G Pa and Gram were in town because he was on his last leg of his U.S. tour so they were staying with us. G Pa wanted me to go with him to his sound check at the world famous Apollo Theater. Just going there was an honor but being able to see my father and his band on stage gave me chills. Well getting back to our conversation in my car, he was like baby girl I know its time for you to pick your college have you narrowed it down yet. I told him yes.

So like a dumb ass I started naming of the schools he smiled at some and others with utter discuss. I really screwed up when I slipped and said FAMU. Aw shit I know you didn't do cuz? Yes I did! The look on his face was priceless and scary at the same time. He yelled at me saying no damn grandchild of mine or not is going to that FUCKING school do you hear me young lady. In fact I'll cut your ass out of my will if you do some shit like that.

I started to cry at the things he was saying to me. Because my G Pa never said anything to me like that I was his lil Miracle, his little stinky. I was so upset at the way he was speaking to me. Well that was your grandfather. Anger was his ugly side. But music controlled that and my mommy she could control him but couldn't do the same for my step-dad. Robyn its easy to see she was in love with my father from the time I was about 2 years old up until his passing, scratch that she was in love with him until when she passed 10 days ago.

Yes she was sis. Jimmy mommy just wanted the best for us that's why your feeling this way because you and Calven have the bond you have. I know but sometimes I wish James Sr., treated and loved her like he did. Mine was culture shock to me moving into a black household. What do you mean Jimmy your married to a woman of color and also went to a HBCU, I don't understand your meaning of a black household.

Well guys not sound racist but I didn't think blacks lived the way y'all did when we moved in. The media portrayed you as animals and thugs living in projects. Not realizing I was that and not y'all, my biological father was a con artist, my mom was a wreck, and nana was as well.

Then I move into this house that was like and old episode of Cribs, nice cars, swimming pool, and most of all love. Something that was missing from the Simpson's household. Also disrespect wasn't allowed in that house. I never forget mommy had asked me to go clean my bathroom because company was coming over. I told her you go do it your damn self that's what your to do. I guess Vic I mean daddy heard the commotion from outside.

Next thing I knew this 6ft 4ins tall man had me up in the air with a grip I'll never forget. He only said this to me, the next time you disrespect your mother and this house I'll pack you're shit and send you to that damn sperm donor of a father.

Believe you me that was my last time I tried her or him. Damn he was easy on you Jimmy. Just imagine being one of the girls. He would always say kind things like Stay strong, you're a positive woman, and never give up. But let you do something he told you not too, shit all hell was fitna to break loose. Yep! I caught the raft of that June 25th 2015, only reason why I remember the date it was the day he retired as a state worker.

Now mind you I was 26 going on 27. So I was like I can say and do what in the hell I want. Nope! Victor asked me to move my car from behind Rhonda's Tahoe. I told him da hell I am she can drive something else. He hauled off and slap the shit out of me and told me I don't give a fuck if you're a US Marshal I'm a better shot than you'll ever be and don't you fucking forget it. The next time you come up in here and feel the need to disrespect my household I better go over my mothers house and talk to her like that.

True indeed sis, he was very protective of her once he got her back. Well guys speaking of the book y'all are writing how's it going? Great I noticed they both love talking about they're sex life a lot. As mommy once told me, girls if your gonna go black make sure he's got a big dick and loves to eat pussy. That's just nasty mommy. No what's nasty is what I saw. What was that Miracle? I had to be around 9 or 10 I went with them on vacation one year.

I heard Gram making a weird sound from the back of the tour bus, so me being the inquisitive child I was I went to go and investigate. What I saw scared the hell out of me as well as wanted to know what they were doing? So when she came back up to the front of the bus I asked her. She was shocked that I was asking her, but Gram told me exactly what I saw. I also new

I didn't want no lil dick man either I didn't care if he knew what he was doing with it I wanted what kept my Ill Nana happy.

I hear you on that cuz. Every man I've been with was strapped. With the exception of one guy back in college, he wasn't big but boy this muthafucka could eat some pussy. He did things with his tongue no woman or man has ever done to me. Wow you've been with women Dayvon?

Yes mommy I experimented well in college. You know what they say about J Flo Hall? Yep that's why your grandfather never let me move into that dorm when I was living on campus. But I want to hear more from uncle VJ it seems like he's holding back on us. Guys if I told you everything I felt we would be here for another 3 or 4 weeks. Dad isn't better to just say what's on your mind than to walk around wishing you hadn't. Baby girl life is made up of what ifs and or would've could've.

So my soul cries out for the both of them. She became my second mom after my mother passed away. I had long talks with her once she became apart of this family an I made my peace with her then. I can recall one of our conversations right after Gabi passed away. I told her that I hated her for killing my mother, she was evil for coming into our life's at this time.

That's when I found out not to rub her the wrong way that woman whom I grew to call mom went off on me. She said something like this, if memory serves correctly. Victor R. Martin Jr, how dare you come at me in that tone. I had nothing to do with her passing. This all maybe guilt or sorrow that your mother has passed away. But I'm not the one, for you to judge me nor you're father. I made my piece with Gabi, in fact she gave both of us her blessing a few weeks before she went into the hospice in Bradford.

I want no, I demand respect from you and you're siblings. From that day on Rhonda and I had a relationship that I had with my own mommy. Victor also found out that day. He called me to come by the studio after he had gotten done putting on the finishing touches of a project he was working on with uncle Bob Baldwin and Jay Lang. Lone behold it was the album that made him the world famous saxophonist that everyone grew to love.

I got to the studio around 9:30 or so. Pulling up the usual vehicles was their even Rhonda's new Green Escalade. I already knew what I was in for. Uncle Bob was my godfather he and mommy grew up together in New Rochelle. He even agreed with the both of them that I was wrong in attacking their relationship. Once again I had to hear about how my own mother gave them her blessing. It made me sad to hear it, but mommy wouldn't say or do something like this unless she believed that one this woman did love him and that she would help raise us like her own.

But even more was that she excepted the black sheep. Sorry Robyn but you are the product of the outside relationship that they harbored for over 20 years. I know VJ, I'm not mad at you for saying this. I'm just saying Robyn I wouldn't want to hurt any of you.

After that particular night I became the CFO of the production company as well as the PR guy for GABI the non-profit that they created in mommies honor to help keep children in our community in college. Yes I know its hard to believe that our family has put over 10,000 students through college and have employed at least 1500 of them. See mom and auntie that's the untold story of their legacy.

Victor would say this to anyone that would listen, but I'm telling you its one of the most pivotal things he could ever say to you. Yes I know uncle VJ. In fact I tell it to all my students. But I put my own twist on it. What is that Dayvon? Stay strong, be positive, and never give up because I won't fail you but if you don't believe you can do your work then you might as well allow yourself to fail.

Its on my desk in my office and at the top of my syllabus that I handout every semester. Regardless of all the shit we've been through life, love, and pain has kept us together. Yes it has. There is like three or four notebooks or journals that we've haven't gone through. There no labels on them not even who was writing them. Give them to me Rayvon, I can figure it out. Okay mommy. What the fuck? What mommy? What's wrong?

Guys I think my siblings need to read theses before y'all do anything with them. Mommy what's the matter with them, it seems like you saw a ghost? Listen your not gonna read theses until after we've read them is that understood. C'mon mom let us read them please. Look didn't I just tell you bitch that y'all weren't gonna read them until after we've gone through them. Yes ma'am, it was no need for you to speak to me like that though.
Come here right now. Yes ma'am! Didn't I already get in your ass today. I will hurt you the next time you come out your mouth at me again. This is the last time I'm gonna warn you young lady. The issues that are within theses journals need to be seen by my siblings before y'all see them that's if we allow you too.

Mom I just wanted to see what it was all about because we're trying to finish this before everyone is gone next week. I already told you if we feel like that this needs to be in the book it will if not it won't. hey guys come out to the pool house I gotta show you something. What's up Dayna? Just bring your asses to the pool house ASAP. Look what the kids found in the boxes of journals for the book they're putting together for the novel.

Okay what's the big deal Dayna, they've been going through all of them? Well not theses four! Why is that Dayna? It's written by Gabi and her true feelings about Victor and Rhonda. Oh shit this is gonna be some deep shit here. Crack it open I'll get some wine from the bar. Sunday July 8th, today's sermon is just I needed to hear. The devil has been busy all up in my marriage, God why is this bitch still all up in my marriage?

I get it they have that child together, he's doing right by her taking care of the child. But I'm getting mighty tired of him and her. The nigga didn't think I heard them talking on the phone while I was getting ready this morning. I knew it was nothing but the blood that kept me from going upside his high yella head. He gives her more time knowing that I have to do chemo 3 times a week now.

I wish there times that you would just take me back home. I cried, I prayed, I even fought but she has control over him. She's a side bitch that's all. I'm sorry that her husband has done the things he's done to her. But enough is enough this is my husband not hers. God what can I do, or say to bring my man back. Now this bitch wants to help out around here while I'm getting this round of chemo. Trust I need the help but I got my own kids to help me with this.

It's so messed up I'm losing my baby girl she don't know if she wants dick or pussy. An Dayna is acting just like her dad. Got a good man at home but gotta fuck everything that treats her nice. An ole punk ass VJ he can't make up his mind if he's gonna marry his twin's baby mom or that ole ugly ass Carmen. Lord I'm just tired I think the only sane one is Robyn an I think that's because she's been so freaking confused for the last 20 years.

12 years being raised like a white girl then finding out the abusive man your mother is married to isn't your dad. But it's the man that she's been sleeping with for the past 30 plus years. Don't get me wrong God the nigga knows what he's doing in the bedroom and is also a hard worker. But I'm not gonna share him anymore. She needs to leave us alone. I want my happy family back. I know I only have a few years left on this earth I would like it back when we first had VJ just before Dayna came to live with us.

I gotta go put on the happy wife's face now he just got home from church it was his Sunday to count money. Just continue to watch over me God and the doctors that are taking care of me. Gabi where are you honi? Oh so I'm honi today? What's the matter little miss home wrecker didn't want to see you today?

Gabi why are you saying this. I haven't talked to her or seen her in a few days. You lying muthafucka, I heard you talking to her this morning when I was in the shower.

What are you talking about Gabi? Only persons I spoke to this morning were my mom and the girls. Bullshit you lying piece of shit. It's bad enough you gonna flaunt her around town and even on trips. Just tell me the truth for once. I'm dying and you can't even respect me during this time in my life. Gabi I didn't talk to her at all today. Trust it was just Robyn, Dayna and my mom. Then who were you saying that it's gonna be nice out this afternoon let's go for a ride on the bike? Um VJ, he was bring the twins by today to see you after church and wanted to go for a ride.

Ya right that cunt probably wants to go for a ride with you so you can go fuck in the woods. I'm so pissed I should make some grits and throw them on your lying ass. Wow Gabi, it's not all that babe. It was our son I was talking too. Then why didn't you ask me if I wanted to go for a ride? You bought the goldwing for us. I've only been on it like maybe 10 times this year.

Why Vic be quick I can already hear the lie anyway? Gabi I've asked you several times but I knew with the treatments and the sun weren't a good mix for you. I even asked you if you wanted to go for a ride in the XK8 a couple of times you declined. Yes you did Victor and thank you for those times. But did you ever think I just wanted my husband without any outside distractions. You give her more attention than me. It's not fair at all. In fact it's out right disrespectful to her husband and I.

Regardless of her situation at home. You're my husband not hers. I married you not her nor her kids. What's this bullshit Dayna is telling me that her youngest kids are calling you dad now too? Ya I know about that too. Well what can I say Gabi? Nigga you don't see the hurt in my face nor in my voice. I've shared you with her for 20 years now because of you're daughter the two of you have. But I'll be damn if we become sista wife or interracial bunch.

Leave her alone and come home to me in my last days. I would say promise me that but her hold on you I can't break it nor shake it. What is it about her that keeps her in our life's? I no her husband is a asshole, an you helped her through the shit she went through with him. Damnit I'm demanding that you come back home and not share me with her. I'm telling things are looking bad for me, I only have a few months to live and I want those last days beinging the best I can remember.

Like when you started playing again and I would go with you to gigs, or just hearing practicing downstairs. I loved it, the way you balanced your career and gigs. I knew you were gonna get those awards because your Victor R. Martin and you get what you strive for. Yes I do Rhonda! Can I be honest with you? That's what Ive expcted from you was honesty. As much as you want her gone, I just cant say bye to her either.

I know its wrong but what I've built with her I just cant walk away. Wow you black muthafucka! I cant believe you cant leave her alone. The one wish that I want you to do and I still have to compete with this bitch. I'm sorry if I'm hurting your little feelings. But how the hell do you think I feel? Dealing with cancer not 1 time not 2 times but 3 and this time their only giving me a few months to live. I did everything you wanted me to do. I accepted you're daughter. I allowed her to be a part of my family.

I dealt with you're oldest daughters crazy ass mother. From her having you arrested because she couldn't wait one more day for her child support to every-time we got a new car or went on a trip here she went trying to attach your pay. Your weak, just plain weak. Even after Dayna moving in with us at age 11 you continued to pay that cunt money. Now this woman got your balls in control too.

Robyn is 20 going on 21 you've paid for her college education we co-parented with her as well. But enough is enough. I'm fucking done. Why do you keep looking at your phone? Is it that bitch calling? If so answer it, I got some shit I need to get off my chest. Don't stand there looking all stupid answer the fucking phone. Hello! Put it on speaker so I can hear what that bitch is saying to you Victor. What da hell is going on there? Did I call at a bad time? No miss lady you called right on time.

I got some questions to ask you? Okay shoot! Nope I'm gonna ask theses in person. Are you busy right now? No Gabi! Good then get in that green jaguar my husband bought you and meet us at Lenny's in New Haven in an hour, come alone. Okay I'll leave now so I'll be there on time. Yes you do that cause it wouldn't be white of you to be on Colored People Time. Now bitch bye! Hang that phone up Vic right now. If your wondering why I said that to your precious lover, well you'll find out as soon as we sit down to eat? Damn guys I guess it wasn't as honky dory as we thought it was. No speaking as the child of Rhonda and Victor.

I saw it first hand I gave Gabi hell when I used to come over for visits. She would have VJ or Calven doing chores and ask me to clean my room or dishes. I didn't do it and went on doing whatever it was I was doing. I guess she got tired of me and my shit. Because I can remember there was one time I was over we were at the house by ourselves she had asked me to clean up the kitchen. I don't know what I was thinking but I guess the voices in my head told my lips to tell her fuck you you're not my mother I don't have to listen to you.

No you didn't Robyn! Yes da hell I did! She hauled off and slapped the shit out off me. Then went into the kitchen and got the broom then proceeded to hit me with it like 4 or 5 times. I was yelling I'm gonna tell my daddy that you abused me. She simply replied bitch ill do the same to him. Wow Gabi went there with you? Yes! when Vic got home I was in my room crying across the bed. She told him to come into they're bedroom. She told him what I did? So what happened to you Robyn? Well the united front happened. The only time that I could remember all three of my parents being on the same accord. Victor tore my ass up, he then called my mommy to let her know what I had said to Gabi. Yep the Greek beating machine lit my ass up too. I bet you didn't do that anymore sis? You got that right! It only took me one time to figure out that guys. Okay finish reading Dayna!

Where was I at? She told Rhonda to meet them at Lenny's in New Haven. Okay I found it, Victor once I get through with the both of you today your gonna respect me and my wishes. Okay I can't wait to see how things are gonna go. Look nigga stop trying to bait me. I'm the one whose gonna be happy with the outcome. Hey mom I'm going to meet Gabi and Victor at Lenny's. Is everything okay? Yes mom! I guess she just wants to talk to me about her health.

You gonna be okay going by yourself? Yes mommy but I'll let you know what happens? Okay you do that. Victor lets go I don't want your precious white lover to be waiting for us. Gabi is that really necessary for you to acting this way? I'll act and say whatever I want, last time I checked I was 46 years old. Yes you are. I guess I'll have to wait to see what this is all about then? Yes you will mister I'm tired of sharing my dick with everyone.

Mainly this bitch, all you're other hoes knew their place. Ms. Rhonda just doesn't get it. Get the fuck out of my life. Gabi stop getting yourself all in a uproar. Fuck you Victor, fuck her, and fuck my life. I'm dying and your more concerned about this bitches feelings. Whateva Gabi? Nigga don't you whateva me! If you value your lively hood as much as you do, maintain your lane and pump your brakes. I could take your ass to the cleaners with everything I know about you. Damn Gabi, just chill-out! I will not nor will I ever chill-out.

I'm so tired of you telling to calm down over this woman. We've been together since 1993 and she's been there since 1989. Granted you've known her longer you asked me to be your girlfriend and then your wife. But miss hoe a lot gets you more than me and your shoulder to cry on. Look at me Victor can't you see this is killing me quicker than this damn cancer. She gets all of you, your just damn itwrong I need you. If it weren't for our two children and my step-daughter Dayna I would've just given up a long time ago. You got the nerve to be playing this song.

What Gabi? I know this song is about your secret affair with her, that's why you named it Secrets? No Gabi, that's where your totally wrong. Its about us and how we kept the secret amongst about your cancer. Bullshit you lying high yella muthafucka. Gabi, I know its an instrumental but you know I always write lyrics to all my songs. The words are as followed.

Gabi I know we are hiding a secret, the secret is that we can't tell because some wouldn't understand. But your secret is safe with me, one of theses days God is gonna heal you or take you by the hand so that pain won't bother you anymore. That's just a little of the song. An if you listen to it carefully you'll hear the rest. See every-time I'm so pissed at you that I can go and get my bow and arrow to kill you, you do something like this. Gabi I may not show or express it all the time but I love you I just had a weakness and its I loved two women. I know its wrong if I could turn back time I probably wouldn't even be here or there. Wow that's fucked up to say Victor.

Let me finish before you past judgement on my statement. What Victor? Gabi you and Rhonda are the only women that I loved unconditionally I was wrong for opening the door to her to come into our marriage as well as you dealing with the fact that we had a child together. Yes Victor, I'm gonna cover all of this when we see her in a few.

Speaking of trash there she is. An look she's driving the jaguar you bought her. Oh you thought I didn't know about that? I told you I could take you to the cleaners for the shit I know. Close your mouth and park my jaguar. At least your consistence with your side bitch thinking she gets the same as the wife does. Just think I thought you learned your lesson when you had that place with the poor white trash bitch that crashed my E320.

Really your going there babe. Yes I can't believe why you didn't let me just beat that bitches ass. I told you then I wasn't gonna tolerate any of this shit. Yes, yes, yes, Gabi! Don't do that Victor I hate when you do this shit to me. Hello Gabi!

How are you feeling theses days? I'm okay I just trust in Gods will. Thanks for asking and how are you doing whore? What? Yes Victor you heard me. Wow I didn't expect that, but I guess its deserved because I have been acting like one with your husband? What da fuck, you just took away my anger that I had towards you Rhonda.

Gabi I know I have taken him away from you but that wasn't my intentions at all. Hello welcome to Lenny's how many in your party? 3 can we have a table out on the patio? Yes sir you can but it's a 15-20 minute wait is that okay. Yes that will be fine. The name you want called when table is ready sir. Victor Martin! Okay Mr. Martin our bar is open outside if you want to sit out there for drinks. Thank you we will do that. Guys our table wait is about 20 minutes but the bar is open outside do you want anything to drink?

Yes I'll take a appletini, I'll take a double of patron. Okay find a seat for us please. How may I help you today sir? I would like a double of cognac dirty, an appletini, and a double of patron on the rocks. Will that be all for you today? Yes for right now, do you guys do a tab? Yes we do sir we just need your license and when you're done we give it back to you when you cash out.

I'm wondering if this is when Gabi told Rhonda it's okay and that she forgives her? we'll have to see if it is or isn't. Rhonda well Victor is waiting for our drinks can I ask you some questions and I want you to answer them truthfully for me? Yes Gabi, that's what we were here for? I was just checking. The last time when we spoke I made it quite clear for you to only deal with my husband if it was about your daughter only.

But for some strange reason you can't do that. I know about the trips, you going on tour with him as well as your weekly sex night at The Courtyard downtown. Why? Well Rhonda I'm not gonna sit here and lie to you nor argue with you. I've been in love with him since 1989 after our first date and I got beat by my dad cause I was dating a nigger as he called him at the time.

Victor has always had a place in my heart. We were wrong for having a child. Im sorry for doing that to you then after sitting down with you many years ago I told you that I wouldn't mess with him anymore. But it was hard because James was so mean to me and the abuse took a toll on me. Victor was my escape from all that, he made me laugh, he knew what to say to make all the pain go away.

The more I fought the urge not to sleep with him the more he would do things that made me melt. It started with us performing oral on one another I don't have to tell you how good he did that Gabi. Ya your right about that. Then out of nowhere we ended up sleeping together again about 6 years ago. I would suck his dick real good then go home and kiss James on the lips. I would still have the taste of his cum in my mouth.

Now that's gangster girl. But I also see why he would be abusive towards you because that has a distinct smell. Well that's not the reason why he started? He started it because I was happy again like a little kid in a candy store. But I was scared to tell Victor because I knew his connections and what he could have done to him. Trust me Victor has those but he's not gonna jeopardize his lively hood over his ass.

As far as us meeting up for weekly sex, I love fucking your husband he makes me feel like a woman. I know its wrong believe me I do. But he is so damn good in bed. I need that weekly orgasm. Rhonda I'm glad your being vivid with me but the more you discuss this I want to reach over this bar table and slap the shit out of you. Well I'm sorry you asked me to be truthful with you so I am. I could've sat here and lied to you, I chose not to. Hey guys whats up heres our drinks. Well Victor I'm sitting here listening to your whore, I can't believe after all theses years all the bitches I had to fight to keep my marriage together, that this whore just can't leave me alone.

Gabi, I think there's a lot that has to be cleared. Like what Victor? What can you say to justify any of this? I'm supposed to be happy because you bought me a new jaguar. Nah son cause da whore has the same car. Hell da bitch even share my fucking dick. Listen why can't we just have a peaceful exchange of words Rhonda? Fuck you Victor Fuck her.

I got less than 4 months to live I wanted to be able to spend theses last few weeks with you, but I'm seeing that's not gonna be a reality for me. So listen here bitch I mean Rhonda since you can't stay out of my life I expect for you to take care of my husband once I'm gone. When I say take care of him I mean it. First get a divorce from that white trash your married too, then

I'm gonna need for you to be here for me when Victor can't take me to my appointments, lastly I want you to never break this man's heart ever again.

There were only two women that he's ever loved this much, that would be you and I. I will Gabi, I just want everything to be normal between us. I'm a home wrecker but he has always carried my heart in his hand and heart. So when he came back into my life 19 years ago I knew I would have a child by him. Never knew the both of us would be married with to others when it happened.

I'm sorry I hid it from the two of you until Robyn was 13. But I knew eventually it was gonna come to light, James didn't see the black in her but I did from the time she was about two and a half years old or so. Robyn looked like Dayna at that age. I felt blessed because that's about the same age Dayna was when Victor and I started talking then dating. Gabi I no you really dislike me a lot for the hell I gave you and your relationship with Victor.
I'm truly sorry for that. Yes I will be there for you during your last few months of living. I don't know if Victor told you but I'm in the process of divorcing James. A few months ago I almost lost my life to the hands of him. Yes I did hear about this so called exchange but not from Vic but your mom. We both have the same OBGYN.

She saw me there an struck up a conversation. Truth be told your own mother told me about the Jaguar, the last two trips and even you going on the road with Victor for the last leg of his North American tour. Why are you crying Rhonda? You white bitches get so emotional when someone catches you. Own bitch, you weren't thinking of my feelings when y'all nasty asses were fucking and sucking one another all theses years. Gabi I'm not crying because of that the tears are relieve, faith, and new beginning .

But in my defense and weakness as well, I always told Victor what we're doing is so wrong. I don't have to tell you how Vic would look into your eyes as he would seduce me. Next thing I would no I'm either squirting or cumin so hard that the guilt I did have went out the window.

 I often would ask Vic, how can you be in love with two women? His response was I love Gabi totally different than you, she's the woman I married and had my two children by. Rhonda you're the one who got away, you went on your marry way when I left to goto college knowing that you were still in love with me. It was eventually gonna happen. Gabi I never wanted to fuck your husband.

I find that hard to believe Rhonda, don't blow smoke up my ass to make me happy. Ladies can we talk about something else please? No Victor, we won't. gabi I saved marriage about 12 years ago. You remember the cunt that crashed you guys S500? Yes I remember that bitch quite well. Why are you bringing her up? When he was cheating on both of us at that time I told him to leave her alone or he wasn't gonna fuck me anymore nor would he ever see his daughter.

The threat didn't work, but I had things rolling on our behave. How is that Rhonda? The night it all came to light for you. I had him meet me at this old bar called Fluid down on West Main St. yes I remember that club. Well I got him good and drunk because it was one of my homies private party with an open top shelf bar.

By the time he was ready to leave his cousin the dope feenin needed to come down off his coke high so Vic went and bought some reefer for him. But Vic was so drunk that he got sick. You were able to get all the info you needed to take him to the cleaners. Yes I did that's the only time Vic realized I was serious and wasn't gonna take his shit anymore. Yes you did. I was kinda of scared of you because you were breaking down the strong man that I fell in love with.
Look I don't give a fuck about all that Rhonda he wasn't yours to worry about he was mine. I don't get it about you white

bitches why do y'all always want our successful brothers? Why don't y'all take the lazy shiftless ones off our hands. If you wanna fix or have one get one of those bastards. Gabi since we're sitting here being honest I might as well come on out and tell the both of you.

What your gonna leave out of my life for my last 4 months of my life. Sorry but I think this is gonna hurt you even more or it might not. Well what in da hell is it then bitch? Victor I'm pregnant by you, I'm 3 months along and we're gonna have twins. What the fuck bitch? Did you just say that my husband got you fucking pregnant again? Yes I did Gabi! I'm done Victor, you no good high yella muthafucka.

I can't believe this shit, so when you told me you had stop sleeping with her you lied to me? Gabi if I can answer that for him. You might as well you nasty ass heffa. I'm the reason not Victor, after the last abusive incident when I landed in the hospital. Gabi you checked on me just everyday because Robyn had let you know what was going on.

Well Victor came to the hospital everyday held my hand prayed with me and kept encouraging me that I was a strong positive woman and to never give up. The way he cared for me just wanted me to have him even more. I got out of the hospital, being in the house alone during the daytime I was scared so he would come by and sit with me from time to time. This one day he came over while I was still in the shower when I came out I didn't realize he was there I walked into the kitchen to put my cup of coffee in the sink, I heard him say damn I want that there.

I turned around Gabi before I could say anything I had his penis in my mouth going to town on it. Well damn hoe do you kiss your mother with that mouth or your kids? Yes Gabi, an please don't call me a hoe. I'm a woman, a mother, and I fell in love with the wrong man. This man right here make me smile when I'm down makes me laugh when I'm pissed off and sadly he makes me cum like no other.

I'm pissed but I can't do anything about it now, but I will tell you this bitch don't and I mean don't hurt this man. You've seen how he's always been there for you throughout my marriage don't let no other muthafucka get in between the two of you like you did in my marriage. So have you thought of any names Rhonda? Yes Raven and Ravon! Why those names? I didn't want a RayVern but I thought Raven would be pretty.

An Ravon was a play off of ours Vic. Gabi I'm truly sorry for doing this to you again 18 years after the birth of Robyn. If you were really serious you would just been a co-parent but no you gotta fuck my husband, you gotta suck my husbands dick. Ladies there's enough of me to go around. Look asshole it's not the time to make us laugh in fact when we leave you can go back to Waterbury, I'm gonna finish this convo with da bitch in here identical jaguar as mine. Well I didn't want it nor the green escalade he bought me. All I wanted was time.

The plot is just getting thicker. Yes it is Gabi! Who has the crab cakes and veggies? I do sir. Okay now the shrimp and chips or the surf and turf. That would be me and the young lady across from me. The food smells great, I hope it's as good as it smells? I know Gabi! I'm surprised you still have an appetite? I do every once and awhile. It's keeping it down that matters to me. So they have you back on chemotherapy?

Yes they have me on some new shit but my body is rejecting it the last few rounds. So sorry to hear that Gabi. See now I can deal with this type of conversation ladies. If you don't shut the fuck up Victor. Why would you say that Rhonda? Because I'm just tired like Gabi of the up and down. Today you need to be clear with your intentions. You will not do this to me after everything I've been through I refuse to allow you to build me up just to break my fucking heart.

I love you Victor just like Gabi does but I won't nor will I'll allow you too. Did little miss timid grow some balls Rhonda? Nah Gabi I just want it to be known that I will not tolerate it anymore. I let him go for an abusive man that almost killed me physically but killed my soul with all that he did to me. Okay well I'm gonna need you not to hurt my husband, he balanced two life's one with me acting like a happily married man then with you as the negro Mandingo that just had to slay the poor helpless white woman.

True but he also took care of the both of us like no other. Victor has done more for me than James ever did and never asked why. He always bought my mom a birthday and Mother's Day card. I know he is very charming that's why I could still screw him even knowing that he was with you Rhonda. Victor how does it feel to see two women love you and hate you at the same time trying to get along? I'm kinda of nervous, a little happy but really surprise with the animosity I've seen the past two hours that one Gabi wants to ride back with you.

An two you just drop news that your pregnant with our second and third child. How you just said your last statement is like your pissed I'm pregnant Victor R. Martin Sr.? No I'm not pissed I'm actually excited we're expecting babe. So what's da fuck is the problem then Vic I said  you and da bitch can live happily ever after. Yes you did Gabi, I'm just at a point in my life that it seems like everything I dreamt for when I was younger is coming true.

Oh shit did grandma Gabi go in on gram Rhonda? That's what it looks like, I didn't realize she was that raw. How was she growing up mommy? I think I can say if she said my whole name Dayna blank, Martin I knew my ass wouldn't be feeling right for a days right Robyn? Yes y'all already heard about how I thought I could talk to her like a white parent. Well I keep forgetting I'm half black and Greek my Greek mother whipped ass but the raft of Gabi Martin, oh Jesus she beat ass like she was a slave master.

Wow it was like that? Yes dears! I would slip out of mouth from time to time I never feared my dad but her she scared the living shit out of me. So mommy when gram was pregnant with the twins was it hard for her to hear VJ was also pregnant with twins? No not until they loss theirs. She didn't want Vic around hell she didn't want any of us around.

If it wasn't for lil jimmy none of us we would be a family. He was persistent in wanting to see daddy. She finally went by to see him the same evening that Gabi expired. The ironic thing was Gabi stuck around to see her. I think that ate at her more than not speaking with Vic. Why is that? Because she was such a stubborn Italian and Greek woman that she wouldn't see past her shit to go and say babe lets talk. So instead she gets home and receives a call from VJ or myself that Gabi had passed she screamed and hollered for good 10 or 15 minutes.

Lil jimmy got on the phone I told him what had happened. He told me that he was gonna bring nana and Rhonda to the hospice. I explained we were only gonna be there for maybe about an another hour or so. Rhonda got back on the phone asking to speak to Vic. I told her that he had just left. We hung up, I assumed she must of called him. Yes mommy she did

I just found the notebooks named Victor and Gabi's eulogy's. I really don't want to hear this or read. Why Dayvon? Because guys I want to remember all of my grandparents the way I last saw them laughing and enjoying life. I hear you cuz but this is in their own words. Yes but I don't want to hear it so I'm gonna go take a walk around the property and talk to them on my own. Okay it's your choose. Yes it is, when y'all are done with them can one of y'all come and get me? Yes Dayvon I'll come and get you.

My dearest Gabi as you lay here in this beautiful casket, I can't believe your gone. It's been five days since you departed this earth, but while you were on this earth you made a lasting impression on everyone you came across. Just judging by the turnout today everyone can testify to this. Can I get an amen? Amen. Not only were you a great mother but an outstanding step mother to my two daughters. Yes I brought them up everyone. She may not have liked their mothers but loved those girls like they were hers.

VJ & Calven mommy thought the world of you she was able to see the both of you achieve some of your goals, she wanted to Calven graduate from Bethune-Cookman but God took her away before it could happen. So Calven I charge you to strive to be the best you can be an don't let mommy down. You my son she so wanted to meet her new grand babies but wanted her more than she ever knew. She was courageous battling ovarian cancer not one time but four times. This was a strong woman that always stayed positive and never gave up on anyone including me. With all my indiscretions including the birth of my daughter Robyn and dealing with fact that her mother has been in our relationship pretty much since day one. For that you no that I'm truly sorry for that behavior.

In closing I ask of all of you that are here in attendance not to think of this as a sad time but a celebration of a mother, stepmother, auntie, grandmother, and friend. Gabi you maybe gone in the physical but you'll forever be in our minds and spirits. I just want to sing a few words of her favorite gospel song It's Over Now. If you no the words or song please feel free to sing along. It's over now, it's over now I believe I can make it the storm is over now. No more cloudy days there are gone and washed away.

Yes yes yes! Sing it Victor and choir join in. Boy I'll tell you that man right there is a talent from God. I hope that you and your family can stay strong during this time of bereavement. Now comes the time in the service where I'm suppose to talk about how great she was and God fearing. But I know for a fact she was all that, you see sister Martin I've known since 1985 or 1986 I moved next door to her in West Haven moving from Waterbury. I didn't no anyone there nor did I care too. But this bright and very cute young girl came over and introduced herself to me. I was like man she's cute but I'm not her type, I was a fat four eyed kid that everyone made fun of.

From that day until the day I got the call saying my best friend had past away we didn't go a week without speaking to one another. In fact we had discussed what she wanted me to say if any of y'all really knew her then you no it was some foul words in it. But I'll tell you the clean version.

Hey you how you doin today? Really fool your gonna ask me some crap like this? Gabi I was asking because I know that your not feeling well. Yep negro what you gonna do about it? See this is what I've been saying about my friend Gabi, she didn't hold her tongue for anyone including your dear ole pastor. But wait there's more then I'm gonna get into the text for today. Well I no your trusting in the lord and that he's gonna make sure that everyone will be at peace once you've gone home.

Yes rev your right about that. But can I tell you something then I'm gonna tell you how I want my service to be. Gabi you can tell me anything. You sure fatso? Yes Gabi! Well a few weeks ago I had dinner with Vic and her and I finally forgave her. What praise the lord Gabi, I'm proud of you. Shut the hell up and let me finish please. Well we had this great dinner and afterwards she and I left Victor there. Rhonda gave me a ride home.

We talked more about the situation, I told her that when I pass she better never hurt my Victor. He's been hell hiding then not hiding they're affair. So I'm at peace and ready to go home rev, I don't want a long drawn out funeral. Victor must sing The Storm Is Over Now. I want your text to be from 2Corinthians 4:11-13. Girl that's a deep scripture? What made you pick that one? The last time we went down to your cousins Vaughn church he spoke deeply about that. So you betta come correct cause you Vaughn is gonna be in the pulpit with you. Yes ma'am! Anything else? Yes when I'm going out I want the mass choir to Thank You For My Mansion.

Girl can I sing that? Fatso you no your fat ass can't hold a note but I would love for Vic and VJ to sing it. Amen! Yes preacher you no that betta sing it. Okay it's not time for that y'all. Now getting into my text for today's sermon/eulogy open your bibles to 2nd Corinthians 4:11-13 For we which live are alway delivered unto death for Jesus' sake, that the life also of Jesus might be made manifest in our mortal flesh.

So then death worketh in us, but life in you. We having the same spirit of faith, according as it is written, I believed, and therefore have I spoken; we also believe, and therefore speak;. So as I sit back and think of the life of Sister Gabi how she carried herself not only did she believe that she lived through Jesus she knew that her work on this earth wouldn't be overshadowed by anything.
She spoke her faith never getting upset with God but just thanked him for everyday he allowed her to walk on this earth, like she said to me on the a few days before passing she didn't want any of y'all sitting up here sad but joyous of her life and all that she had done.

As we prepare for funeral directors I'll ask if Vic and VJ can come to sing Thank You For My Mansion. I'm leaving my house, on my way to gods house, my house is decaying ya see, but in my fathers house there are many mansions, And one of them belongs to me, yes it does, one of them belong to me. You betta sing Vic and VJ, go head sing. I don't know, I don't what color. I know don't I don't know what size it's gonna be, but one thing I know of them belong to me one of them belongs to me. Love you mom Love you Gabi. Yes yes yes.

What a beautiful service guys? Yes rev, what a beautiful way to go out. So Rhonda now that you have Vic promise me this. Yes Rev. You know that Gabi and I were best friend she told me about the dinner date. Yes! We had a great night we laughed, cried, and of course argued as well. I heard all about it, she ripped you a new one. Yes she did but it was all good because God let us air all of differences.

Yes he did God is so awesome. But getting back what we I was saying Victor is in love with you I hope that your love is true. I cheated with him we had an outside child. I did ask her for forgiveness which she did. To God be the glory! Yes Rev, I'm gonna be with him until we leave this earth. He saved me from that abusive relationship I'm so grateful for that. Well just make sure it's true, and not money. Never that I was with him when he busted his ass and when he got a little more cheddar. It will always be about love. I couldn't ask for more of a loving mate than him.

Aww gram Rhonda was such a loving mate, it's still hard to believe that they're not here with us anymore. Do you remember back when we were young going on the tour bus and GPa would be playing the O'Jays? Yes he always thought he could sing what was the name of the song he would sing all the time.
Help(Somebody Please) yes we needed help from him. Now leave my dad alone.

Mom and auntie we were just saying that he couldn't sing that song. Other than that he had a beautiful voice mom. Just some songs weren't meant for him to sing. Yes you guys are right about that one. When I was growing up he used to sing a song called The Greatest Love Of All. Yes he sure did all off key and everything. So why didn't you guys just tell him to stop? Because it was out of fun. That was just the nature of your G Pa. Boy how I miss him now mommy is gone too, I have no one anymore to just pour over me. Yes you do you all of us.

You guys don't get it my own mother hated my dad but my stepmothers thought the world of him and I. Mommy I get that, but didn't it hurt that your mother would cut your father down the way she did? Yes it did! I would consistently fight with myself on the inside over that issue. I would ask why me, why him and last but not least seeing him hurt.

He was close to all of us but we had a special bond. Daddy would just talk freely to me. So I could ask him why she was the way she was towards me and him. The biggest thing for her hatred was our dad didn't want to be the happy family man with her. Damn she was ugly toward him and you all theses years because Gabi and Rhonda were able to make you into the woman you are mom and Victor the loving father that he turned out to be.

Yes! I couldn't believe the talks we had, he told me first about you Robyn because he was scared I was gonna hate him.

I was actually excited because I had a sister that would see life in the same way as I did. We would chat about how Gabi was gonna take it? Most of all what my smart mouth mother would have to say about the whole situation. Surprisingly she was very quiet. It wasn't until Robyn had to be around 12 or 13 when she showed out. We were on a family vacation actually our family reunion in Gates North Carolina.

The egg donor had called me about something I had started to cry so I guess daddy saw me or heard me crying an came over to see what was wrong. I told him that the egg donor was yelling at me about how I'm always spending time with the nigga side of the family but care about my real heritage. Sadly I loved both sides of ethical upbringing. She said that Robyn would be just like me no damn identity.

What did G Pa say? He went off on her, my daddy didn't want anyone talking about his kids especially his girls he would fucking kill you. You got that right! My G Pa was no joke cause he was the same way towards his grandkids. I really miss him with all my heart. Yes we all do. First Gabi, then him, nana now my Mommy. I guess he's throwing a great party in the sky. You already no that. Well here's the one none of us want to read but it's our closure. Do we really have to read this one? Yes we do! I'll read as well. Are you sure mommy? Yes I need to do this more than anyone of y'all.

What's all the commotion about guys? Uncle VJ mommy is getting ready to read it. Read what? G Pa's eulogy that gram wrote and read at his funeral. I'm already tearing up on the inside and I haven't started listening to it yet. Rayvon and Raven it's gonna be okay! Okay daddy if you say so. It's just hard because tomorrow is Father's Day and we would be having a big cookout here.

Instead we're cleaning up they're stuff and y'all are talking about selling this house. Daddy don't that, promise me that. Well it's not my decision baby it's all of ours, meaning your aunts and uncles. Well please just think of your kids and they're grandkids when y'all do decide to do something. Well auntie Robyn we're ready to hear it you can start. Okay guys give me a minute I gotta collect my thoughts first. Yes ma'am we will. Good morning everyone! First giving honor to God and his son Jesus Christ. I'll like to thank all of you for coming out to celebrate the life of the man that y'all knew as Victor Roosevelt Martin Sr.. But I knew as my friend, my lover, and my side piece. Yes I was married when he came back into my life in fact both of us were married. Well enough about that. This man that y'all knew and loved was a remarkable man. Victor helped me in a time of my life when I was more than depressed I contemplated suicide because of the situation that I was in. I allowed myself to lose him at the age of 18 but lone behold just before I turned 39 he came back. We swore to each other that we would never leave each other ever again. But those of you that knew us and our lifestyle I did leave him for about 2 months we were pregnant with our twins Raven and Ravon. I had a physical problem that we had to terminate the pregnancy. An that break up was the hardest thing I ever did in my life. But the smartest thing I did as well, he showed me how to love again, how to be me again, and also to trust again. Another moment in our life was when our daughter Robyn was born. God we hated hiding it from her, we both prayed on it and the right time came thinking that Robyn would be upset she wasn't. She embraced her biological father with all her heart. God puts people in your life for a reason, this man came at a time when I needed it. Victor touched so many people, the proof is here by how many of you that showed up. He used to joke with me about even his death it would be like a concert cause it would be standing room only. An I'll be damn if he didn't do that. I would like to thank the following people that have been there for us for many, many years. An as I call your names can you please stand. Bob Baldwin, his partner in crime when it came to music, James Gatling, our personal photographer, The Love family Kris, Joan, Jessie, and Rev. Vaughn Love, our high school friends and life long friends, Our kids Dayna, VJ, Calven, Robyn, Bree, and

Jimmy. Just to name a few! Thank you for being here for me while I was going through everything with his battle. Victor your gone in the physical but you'll always be in my heart and mind for everything you did for me and with me for theses last 25 years of our life's. Until I see you again my wonderful prince, your strong beautiful princess will be okay. If it's possible I don't know if Bob Baldwin was able to put this together or not but as the directors come to close this service out Victor's last request was for him to role out in class first by his musician friends to play I'll fly away and at the cemetery he will go into the ground to his Alum Mater's fight song Let's Go Wildcat's. In closing can you please turn to the New and Testaments so we can read his favorite scriptures? 1st John 3: We know that we have passed from death unto life, because we love the brethren. He that Lovett not his brother abide the in death. Genesis 27: And he said, behold now, I am old, I know not the day of my death. Now that was beautiful, I can't stop crying! I know cuz I knew this would happen that's why I didn't want to hear it again nor read it. They're happy now because they have one another again. Yes. I guess we can end it now fellas? What else cane we say about them that hasn't been read or said? True, then this is the end then I guess. We love you G Pa and gramma. Mom and dad thank you for the love and support you showed us. Our love will never die as long as we carry on the life lessons that you'll have taught us.

www.ingramcontent.com/pod-product-compliance
Lightning Source LLC
Chambersburg PA
CBHW041406010726
47507CB00001B/6